The Master's Gambit

The Master's Gambit

Matthew Petchinsky

The Master's Gambit: Keys of Eternal Power
By: Matthew Petchinsky

Disclaimer:

This is a fan-made transformative work inspired by the *Doctor Who* television series and the concept of Infinity Stones from the Marvel Universe. It is not affiliated with, endorsed by, or connected to the BBC, Marvel Entertainment, Disney, or any of their subsidiaries or license holders.

All names, characters, and elements from *Doctor Who* and the Marvel Universe remain the property of their respective owners. This book is a creative homage intended for entertainment and imaginative exploration only.

Introduction: The Shattered Multiverse

There is a moment, imperceptible to most, where the fabric of reality shudders—where time, space, and existence itself seem to draw a collective breath before splitting apart. This moment is rare, fleeting, and catastrophic. It is a moment born of impossible forces colliding, a clash that threatens to unmake the very foundations of the multiverse. It begins with whispers of power: fragments of myths, artifacts of unimaginable potency, and a villain's unrelenting ambition to control them all.

The multiverse, an intricate lattice of infinite realities, has always teetered on a delicate balance. Hidden among these realities are the most powerful relics ever conceived—the **Infinity Stones**, six artifacts of raw energy born at the dawn of creation itself, each governing a fundamental aspect of existence: Mind, Space, Reality, Time, Power, and Soul. To wield even one of these Stones is to command an unrivaled force. To wield them all is to possess ultimate dominion.

Yet the Infinity Stones are not alone in their potential to unravel existence. The **Key to Time**, a legendary artifact of Time Lord creation, was designed to maintain universal harmony by channeling time's unyielding flow into order. When whole, the Key to Time is a beacon of balance. But in the wrong hands—or broken into its constituent fragments—it becomes a tool of chaos, its purpose twisted into something malevolent.

What none could foresee was the catastrophic fusion of these relics. In an era long forgotten, the Stones and the fragments of the Key collided in an interdimensional rift, a convergence that shattered the boundaries of space and time. Though scattered across countless realities, their latent power began to hum in unison, creating ripples of destruction that echoed through dimensions. Those ripples have now grown into waves, and with them comes a storm.

At the heart of this storm stands one man—**The Master**.

The Master, a Time Lord whose name evokes fear across galaxies, is driven by a singular obsession: control. To him, chaos is a ladder, and power is a means to his ultimate end—a multiverse reshaped in his image. Where others see destruction, he sees opportunity. For the Master, the fusion of the Infinity Stones with the Key to Time represents not just power, but possibility. With these artifacts, he can rewrite the rules of existence, erasing the failures and betrayals that have haunted his life. He can become a god.

The Master's journey begins in whispers, fragments of ancient knowledge unearthed from forbidden texts, and decoded signals intercepted across timelines. He learns of the artifacts' convergence, their resonance growing stronger as they draw nearer to one another. But the relics are scattered across the multiverse, guarded by temporal storms, cosmic anomalies, and the remnants of civilizations that have long perished.

Even as the Master plots his conquest, another force stirs in the shadows. The **Doctor**, his eternal nemesis and a being of hope where the Master embodies despair, becomes aware of the looming catastrophe. The Doctor knows the stakes all too well. These relics, if united, would grant their wielder the power to destroy not just one universe but all universes. The multiverse itself would bend or break, shaped by the whims of a single individual.

What sets the Master apart from other villains is not just his cunning or intellect but his ability to believe. He believes in the inevitability of his own victory, in his right to dominate. For the Master, this is not merely a game or an act of revenge—it is destiny. He envisions a multiverse reborn under his rule, where his word is law and where the flaws of existence have been eradicated.

But such power does not come without consequence. The fusion of the Infinity Stones and the Key to Time threatens the very foundation of reality. The multiverse, once an endless tapestry of infinite possibilities, now shows signs of wear. Stars collapse prematurely, timelines fracture and merge, and entire worlds blink out of existence. These are the harbingers of what is to come—a shattered multiverse poised on the edge of annihilation.

As the Master sets his plans into motion, his journey becomes a race against time itself. The Doctor, driven by a relentless hope to save what can still be saved, gathers allies from across time and space. Their confrontation is inevitable, but the stakes have never been higher. For this is no ordinary battle of wills. It is a battle for everything that ever was and everything that could ever be.

In the end, the question is not whether the multiverse will be destroyed. It is who will wield the power to decide what comes after. The Master's dark ambition burns bright, his desire to reshape reality fueled by an ego as boundless as the cosmos. But the Doctor knows there is always another way.

This is the story of their greatest confrontation, where the fate of the multiverse lies in the balance and where the line between hero and villain blurs. This is the story of **The Shattered Multiverse.**

Chapter 1: The Whisper of Eternity

The ruins of the TARDIS floated silently in the void, a shattered fragment of a vessel that once defied time and space. Its metal hull, scorched and broken, drifted through a dying star system, glowing faintly from the radiation of the collapsing star nearby. Inside, however, something still pulsed with life—a faint, rhythmic hum, as though the ship's heart still beat despite its mortal wounds.

For most, such ruins would be a graveyard. For **The Master**, they were an opportunity.

He strode through the shattered corridors of the ancient TARDIS with the confidence of someone who had long ceased to fear the unknown. His black leather coat swept behind him like a shadow, and his eyes glimmered with a dangerous mixture of curiosity and greed.

"Ah," he muttered to himself, brushing a layer of dust off a shattered console. "You may be a relic, but even relics have secrets to tell."

The room was dimly lit by the faint glow of decaying temporal energy. The air crackled faintly, charged with the residue of long-forgotten journeys through time. The Master had tracked the signal to this fragment, a signal that spoke in cryptic whispers through the vortex—a lure he couldn't resist.

As he moved deeper into the wreckage, his footsteps echoed unnaturally, as though the walls themselves were listening. Then he found it: a chamber, remarkably intact despite the destruction around it. In its center, hovering above a cracked pedestal, was the artifact—a sphere of shifting light, its surface rippling with faint images of stars and galaxies.

"Well, aren't you a pretty thing," The Master murmured, stepping closer. His voice dropped, almost reverent. "I can feel it—your power. You've been waiting for someone like me, haven't you?"

The artifact pulsed in response, its light growing brighter.

Suddenly, the silence was broken by a voice, mechanical and ancient. It emanated from a small, battered console nearby.

"IDENTIFICATION REQUIRED."

The Master smirked. "Oh, don't play coy with me. You know who I am."

"IDENTIFY YOURSELF."

Rolling his eyes, The Master stepped forward, placing a hand on the console. "I am The Master, last of the Time Lords you haven't managed to annihilate yet. Satisfied?"

There was a pause, and then the voice returned, quieter this time, almost... hesitant.

"The Master... seeker of chaos. Why have you come?"

His smirk widened. "Seeker of chaos? Oh, I do like that. But no, I'm here for answers. You sent out a signal, and I answered. Now, let's skip the pleasantries and get to the point. What is that?" He pointed to the glowing sphere.

The voice seemed to hesitate again before answering.

"It is... a fragment of the Key to Time. And more."

The Master's eyes narrowed, his curiosity sharpening into something more dangerous. "More, you say? Do elaborate."

"This fragment... fused with another power. A relic from another reality. It hums with the resonance of the six forces: Mind, Space, Reality, Time, Power, and Soul."

For a moment, The Master was silent. Then, slowly, a grin spread across his face. "The Infinity Stones. Well, well. The myths were true after all. And here I thought I'd already seen everything."

The console's voice grew grave.

"The fusion of these forces is unstable. Their power threatens the fabric of existence itself. If reunited, they could unmake the multiverse."

"And remake it," The Master interrupted, his voice low and filled with awe. "That's the part you're leaving out, isn't it? Someone could remake reality in their image."

"Such power is too dangerous to wield."

"Dangerous?" The Master laughed, the sound echoing harshly in the chamber. "Danger is relative. To me, it sounds like opportunity. Tell me—where are the other fragments?"

The console fell silent, as though reluctant to answer. The Master's expression darkened. He stepped closer, his voice taking on an edge. "Don't play games with me. You called me here. You want this as much as I do. Now, where are the fragments?"

The artifact pulsed again, brighter this time, and the console finally spoke.

"The fragments are scattered across the multiverse. Each guarded by forces that seek to contain their power."

The Master's grin returned. "Forces that will inevitably fail, I'm sure. And me? I'll succeed. I always do."

As he reached out toward the glowing sphere, the chamber trembled. Sparks flew from the console, and the light of the artifact intensified, filling the room with blinding brilliance. The Master shielded his eyes but kept moving forward.

"What's this, a warning?" he taunted. "You think a little light show is going to scare me off? Please."

Suddenly, the light coalesced into a single beam, striking The Master's mind like a dagger. Images flooded his thoughts: collapsing stars, shattered timelines, worlds blinking out of existence, and finally, a vision of himself—standing amidst the ruins of a broken multiverse, triumphant.

When the light faded, The Master staggered back, panting. For a moment, he seemed shaken, but then he laughed—a deep, manic laugh that filled the chamber.

"So, that's what's at stake," he whispered, his voice trembling with excitement. "Not just destruction. Creation. A blank canvas for a god. My god."

He turned toward the console, his eyes alight with purpose. "Tell me where to start."

The console hesitated one final time before replying.

"The first lies beyond the rift of Arkadion. A fragment fused with the Mind Stone."

The Master's grin grew wider. "Good. Then it begins. The multiverse doesn't know it yet, but it's mine."

He reached out, took the glowing artifact from its pedestal, and turned to leave. The chamber began to collapse behind him as the temporal energy destabilized, but The Master didn't look back. He had a quest now, a purpose.

The Whisper of Eternity had spoken—and The Master was ready to answer.

Chapter 2: Fragments of the Key

The TARDIS hummed softly as it floated in the serene expanse of the Horsehead Nebula, its blue exterior a stark contrast to the swirling reds and purples of the surrounding gases. Inside, the control room buzzed with life—buttons blinking, levers clicking, and the central console rising and falling in rhythm with the ship's breath. But the Doctor's face was anything but serene.

"Fragments of the Key..." the Doctor muttered, pacing frantically around the console. "Fragments scattered, fused with—oh, this is bad. This is very, very bad."

The TARDIS responded with a low groan, as though agreeing with its pilot's assessment.

"Right," the Doctor said, flipping a series of switches and slamming a lever into place. "First things first: cross-reference all known disturbances in the temporal continuum with residual energy signatures from the Infinity Stones. That should give us a—"

The console suddenly sparked, and a hologram materialized above it—a shifting image of six glowing orbs, each pulsing with a unique light. Surrounding them was an intricate lattice of fragments, their edges jagged and radiating faint temporal energy.

The Doctor froze, staring at the projection. "Oh no. No, no, no. Not the Key to Time. Anything but that."

The hologram shifted, zooming in on one fragment. A faint trail of energy connected it to one of the orbs, the Mind Stone, its light flickering like a distant star. The Doctor's expression darkened.

"Of course, it had to be the Master," the Doctor muttered. "Who else would think it's a good idea to merge the most dangerous artifacts in the multiverse?"

The TARDIS chirped softly, and the Doctor rolled their eyes. "Yes, yes, I know. I'm the only one who can stop him. That's the job, isn't it?

But this—this is bigger than anything he's ever done. He's not just playing with fire; he's throwing matches at a petrol-soaked multiverse!"

Suddenly, the TARDIS console buzzed again, and a voice crackled through the speakers—a distress signal.

"—aid! Anyone who can hear this, please help! He's taken it. He's—"

The signal cut off abruptly, leaving only static.

The Doctor straightened, their face a mix of determination and dread. "Well, that's never a good sign."

The TARDIS hummed again, its lights dimming slightly.

"Don't you start sulking," the Doctor said, patting the console. "We've got work to do. Let's trace that signal."

With a flick of a switch, the TARDIS lurched into motion, its engines roaring as it shot through the vortex. The journey was rougher than usual, as though the universe itself resisted their path.

Moments later, the TARDIS materialized in the ruins of a once-great library, its towering shelves reduced to rubble and ash. The air was thick with the smell of burnt parchment, and the faint hum of residual energy crackled in the distance.

The Doctor stepped out, adjusting their coat and looking around with a mix of curiosity and sorrow. "Ah, the Great Library of Arkadion. Or, what's left of it. Always loved this place. Shame it's been... well, destroyed."

A faint sound caught their attention—a weak groan from behind a toppled shelf. The Doctor rushed over, lifting debris to reveal a battered humanoid figure. Their metallic skin flickered with failing power, their eyes dim but still alive.

"Hello, you," the Doctor said gently, crouching beside the figure. "Let me guess—librarian?"

The figure nodded weakly. "He... he took it."

The Doctor's brow furrowed. "The Master?"

"Yes," the librarian rasped. "The fragment... and the stone. He said... he would remake everything."

The Doctor's jaw tightened. "Of course he did. He always does love a bit of megalomania. Tell me—what did he take, exactly? And where did he go?"

The librarian's voice grew fainter. "The Mind Stone... fused with the fragment of the Key... he said it was the first piece. The others... scattered. Guarded by forces... beyond comprehension."

The Doctor leaned closer. "Do you know where the next one is?"

The librarian shook their head. "The path... it's hidden. Only the Key... reveals the way."

The Doctor sat back, their mind racing. "So he's using the fragments of the Key to locate the other Stones. Clever. Diabolical, but clever."

The librarian's hand weakly grasped the Doctor's arm. "You must... stop him. If he unites them... the multiverse will... fall."

The Doctor's expression softened, and they placed a reassuring hand over the librarian's. "I will. I promise. Just rest now."

The librarian's eyes flickered one last time before going dark, their hand falling limply to the ground. The Doctor stood, a heavy weight settling on their shoulders.

"Right," the Doctor said aloud, addressing the empty library. "No pressure, just the fate of all existence. Again."

They turned back toward the TARDIS, their pace quickening. "If he's already got the Mind Stone and one fragment of the Key, he's one step ahead. Time to change that."

Inside the TARDIS, the Doctor began frantically typing commands into the console. The hologram reappeared, now showing the locations of faint energy signatures across the multiverse.

"There," the Doctor muttered, pointing to a pulsating light on the edge of the projection. "The next fragment. Looks like it's fused with the Reality Stone. Oh, that's just brilliant—warp a little reality while you're at it, why don't you?"

The TARDIS hummed, as though in agreement.

"Hold on, old girl," the Doctor said, gripping the console. "We've got a multiverse to save."

With a pull of a lever, the TARDIS roared back into the vortex, leaving the ruins of the library behind. The Doctor's mind raced with possibilities, strategies, and the lingering fear that this time, even they might be outmatched.

Somewhere, across the infinite expanse of time and space, The Master was already moving. And the Doctor knew they had to catch up—before it was too late.

Chapter 3: Chasing Shadows

The dying star loomed ahead, its light flickering weakly as if fighting a losing battle against the void. Debris from long-destroyed planets floated aimlessly around it, glowing faintly in the radiation of its last gasps. The star system was a graveyard, silent and eerie, except for two ships weaving through its ruins—a blue police box and a sleek black sphere with jagged red accents.

Inside the TARDIS, the Doctor leaned over the console, eyes narrowed as they studied the holographic map of the system.

"Well, this is cozy," the Doctor muttered, flipping switches and pulling levers. "A dying star, collapsing time pockets, and—oh, look! An angry cosmic guardian. Just the sort of place you'd expect to find a fragment of the Key to Time and the Mind Stone."

The TARDIS groaned in response, its lights flickering slightly.

"Don't start complaining now," the Doctor chided, giving the console a reassuring pat. "We've got a head start. Well... maybe not a head start exactly, but we're close! Ish."

As if on cue, an alert beeped loudly from the console. The Doctor sighed.

"Oh, no. Don't tell me it's him."

The scanner screen flickered to life, revealing The Master's ship approaching fast. Its design was unmistakably his—sleek, menacing, and radiating malevolence.

"Of course it's him," the Doctor said, rolling their eyes. "Why wouldn't it be?"

On The Master's Ship

The Master leaned back in his command chair, his expression one of smug satisfaction as he watched the TARDIS on his scanner.

"There you are, Doctor," he purred, his voice dripping with mock affection. "Always showing up just in time to be a nuisance. How very predictable."

He tapped a few buttons on his console, bringing up a holographic projection of the dying star and the fragmented ruins orbiting it. In the center of the chaos, a small object glowed faintly—a piece of the Key to Time fused with the Mind Stone.

"Ah, there it is," The Master murmured, his grin widening. "The first piece of my masterpiece. And I'm not letting you ruin this, Doctor."

He activated his ship's engines, propelling it toward the glowing relic.

Back in the TARDIS

The Doctor slammed a lever, sending the TARDIS careening toward the same destination. "All right, let's see if we can outmaneuver the galaxy's most egotistical Time Lord, shall we?"

The ship jolted suddenly, throwing the Doctor off balance. Sparks flew from the console.

"Oi! What was that?" the Doctor shouted, regaining their footing. They glanced at the scanner and groaned. "Temporal anomalies. Great. Just what we needed."

The TARDIS shook again, harder this time. The Doctor's expression grew serious. "Right, no time to be subtle. Straight through it is!"

The TARDIS roared as it pushed through the swirling chaos of collapsing timelines.

The Relic's Location

The fragment hovered above the star's surface, encased in a shimmering energy field. Its light flickered in rhythm with the dying pulses of the star, as if drawing strength from its impending collapse.

Both ships arrived almost simultaneously, materializing on a large, rocky platform orbiting the star. The Master stepped out first, his presence commanding as he surveyed the relic. Moments later, the TARDIS doors creaked open, and the Doctor emerged, their coat billowing in the intense heat.

"Master," the Doctor called out, voice steady but laced with warning. "You're playing with fire. Again."

The Master turned, his grin widening. "Doctor! So good of you to join me. I was beginning to think you'd lost your touch."

"Oh, you know me," the Doctor replied, walking closer. "Always turning up just in time to stop your latest scheme. But this—this is ambitious, even for you."

The Master gestured toward the glowing relic. "Isn't it magnificent? A fragment of the Key to Time, fused with the Mind Stone. Do you realize the potential here, Doctor? This is more than power—it's destiny."

The Doctor frowned. "It's destruction, Master. You know what happens if you merge these relics. The multiverse isn't a plaything."

"Isn't it?" The Master retorted, his tone sharp. "It's a broken mess, and I intend to fix it. Imagine a multiverse without chaos, without failure. A multiverse shaped by my vision."

"Your vision?" The Doctor raised an eyebrow. "That's not a vision; that's a dictatorship with you at the center. And trust me, the multiverse doesn't need that."

Before The Master could respond, the ground beneath them shook violently. The energy field around the relic intensified, and a deep, resonating voice echoed through the void.

"INTRUDERS. YOU SEEK WHAT CANNOT BE CLAIMED."

Both Time Lords turned to see a colossal figure emerging from the star—a guardian forged of molten light and shadow. Its eyes burned like miniature suns, and its voice rumbled like thunder.

The Doctor sighed. "Brilliant. A cosmic guardian. Because this wasn't complicated enough already."

The Master, however, seemed unfazed. "Step aside, Doctor. I'll handle this."

"Oh, this I've got to see," the Doctor quipped, crossing their arms.

The Master stepped forward, addressing the guardian. "You're guarding something that belongs to me. Stand down, or I'll—"

"YOU ARE NOT WORTHY." The guardian's voice cut him off, its eyes flaring with light.

The Master scowled. "Not worthy? Do you know who I am?"

The guardian raised a massive hand, and the platform began to crumble.

"Master!" the Doctor shouted. "Maybe don't antagonize the giant fiery deity?"

The Master ignored the warning, raising his laser screwdriver and firing a blast of energy at the guardian. It dissipated harmlessly against its molten surface.

"Predictable," the Doctor muttered. They turned back to the TARDIS, grabbing a device from their pocket. "Let's see if we can talk some sense into this thing."

Approaching the guardian cautiously, the Doctor activated the device, emitting a harmonic frequency. The guardian paused, its gaze shifting to the Doctor.

"YOU SPEAK THE LANGUAGE OF BALANCE."

"That's right," the Doctor said, their tone calm. "We're not here to destroy anything. We just want to stop this from falling into the wrong hands."

The Master scoffed. "Don't listen to them. I'm the one with the vision!"

The guardian hesitated, torn between the two Time Lords. The Doctor seized the moment, glancing at The Master.

"Master, we can't fight it. Work with me, just this once."

The Master sneered. "I'd rather face annihilation."

"Typical," the Doctor muttered.

As the platform disintegrated further, the relic's energy field began to destabilize, sending out bursts of raw power. The Doctor dashed toward the relic, narrowly dodging a surge of energy.

"Careful, Doctor!" The Master called mockingly. "Wouldn't want you to get hurt."

"Oh, don't worry about me," the Doctor shot back, grabbing the relic just as the platform gave way entirely.

They scrambled back to the TARDIS, clutching the fragment, while The Master retreated to his ship. The guardian, weakened by the relic's removal, faded back into the star.

As the two ships departed the collapsing system, the Doctor stared at the fragment in their hands, worry etched on their face.

"This is only the beginning," they whispered. "And it's going to get worse."

Chapter 4: The Forgotten Stone

The air crackled with residual energy as The Master's ship materialized on the desolate planet of Varlek IV. Once a thriving hub of innovation and enlightenment, the world now lay in ruins, its great cities reduced to crumbling husks, its population long gone. At the heart of this wasteland was the source of its destruction—a temple of cracked obsidian and glowing fissures, where the **Mind Stone** had embedded itself centuries ago.

The Master stepped out of his ship with his usual confident swagger, his black coat fluttering in the dry, electric wind. He took a deep breath, savoring the air thick with the remnants of power.

"Ah, Varlek IV," he said, his voice echoing across the barren expanse. "A monument to curiosity meeting its inevitable demise. Let's see what secrets you've left behind for me."

The ground beneath his boots crunched as he approached the temple. Lightning arced across the sky, illuminating the jagged architecture. The temple seemed to pulse, as if it were alive, the light of the Mind Stone casting eerie shadows through its cracks.

As he entered, the oppressive silence was broken by faint whispers. Voices. Countless voices, overlapping and fading in and out. The Master smirked.

"Trying to scare me with echoes of the past?" he taunted. "You'll have to do better than that."

The whispers grew louder as he ascended a spiral staircase leading to the temple's core. The closer he got, the more he could feel the Stone's energy, pressing against his mind like a tide threatening to overwhelm him. But The Master was no ordinary being—his mind, sharp and unyielding, pushed back.

Finally, he reached the chamber where the Mind Stone rested. It floated above a cracked pedestal, radiating an intense, golden light. Around it, the remains of Varlek IV's last defenders lay scattered—skeletal figures clutching ancient weapons, their empty sockets staring at the relic that had doomed them.

The Master approached slowly, his eyes fixed on the Stone. "There you are," he murmured, almost reverently. "The power to control thought, to bend wills, to reshape reality itself. And now... you're mine."

As he reached for the Stone, a sudden force stopped him mid-step. A voice, clear and commanding, rang out in his mind.

"WHO DARES CLAIM ME?"

The Master froze, his hand inches from the Stone. He smiled. "Ah, so you can speak. Good. Saves me the trouble of introducing myself. I'm The Master, and I'm here to—how shall I put this?—liberate you."

The voice was cold and unyielding.

"YOU ARE UNWORTHY. LEAVE, OR FACE OBLIVION."

The Master's smile turned into a grin. "Oh, I've faced oblivion before. It's overrated." He reached into his pocket and pulled out the fragment of the Key to Time he had claimed earlier. As its energy resonated with the Stone, the golden light flickered. The whispers in the air intensified, now screaming in anger and fear.

"See?" The Master said, holding the fragment up. "I'm not just some random intruder. I'm here to complete a puzzle, and you're a very important piece."

The Stone's energy surged, but instead of repelling him, it began to pull the fragment closer. The Master stepped forward, his grin widening as he realized the Stone was beginning to accept his claim.

Suddenly, the skeletal remains around the chamber stirred. Empty sockets glowed with the Stone's light as the dead began to rise, their broken bodies animated by its power.

"Oh, now this is interesting," The Master remarked, stepping back slightly. "Unwilling allies, are we? Let's see how far you'll go to stop me."

The reanimated defenders moved toward him, their motions jerky but deliberate. One swung a rusted blade, narrowly missing The Master as he sidestepped.

"Really?" he said, almost laughing. "This is your defense? Zombies with terrible aim? Pathetic."

He raised his laser screwdriver, firing a burst of energy that disintegrated one of the attackers. But for every one that fell, another rose, and the Stone's power continued to build.

"Fine," The Master growled, narrowing his eyes. "If you won't submit willingly, I'll take control myself."

He turned the laser screwdriver to full power, pointing it not at the attackers but at the Mind Stone itself. The energy from the device clashed with the Stone's aura, sending ripples of golden light throughout the chamber. The undead army froze mid-motion, their glowing eyes flickering.

The Master pressed harder, his face strained with effort. "You think you're the only one who can play games with minds? Let me show you what I'm capable of."

The Stone pulsed violently, but the fragment of the Key in his hand began to glow in response, stabilizing the energy. Slowly, the golden light around the Stone dimmed, and the skeletal figures dropped to the ground, lifeless once more.

The Master stepped forward, his hand outstretched. "Now, where were we? Ah, yes. Your new owner."

This time, there was no resistance. The Mind Stone floated into his hand, its surface warm and pulsing with latent energy. As he held it, his mind was flooded with visions—countless possibilities, countless worlds, all bending to his will.

He laughed, a sound that echoed through the empty temple and beyond. "Oh, the things I'm going to do with you."

Suddenly, his communicator buzzed, interrupting his moment of triumph. He pressed a button on his wrist device, and a holographic projection of his ship's control room appeared. One of his robotic servants spoke.

"Master, we are detecting an incoming vessel. It matches the signature of the Doctor's TARDIS."

The Master's grin faltered, replaced by a scowl. "Of course. Right on cue. Well, let them come. I've got what I need."

He pocketed the Mind Stone and strode out of the temple, his coat billowing behind him. As he reached his ship, he glanced back at the ruins of Varlek IV, now silent once more.

"Thank you for your contribution," he said, mockingly bowing toward the planet. "But I've got bigger things to do."

As his ship ascended into the void, the dying star flared one last time, as if in protest. But The Master didn't look back. His sights were set on the next piece of his puzzle—and on the Doctor, who he knew would soon be on his trail.

"Let's see how you handle this one, Doctor," he said, his grin returning. "Because I'm just getting started."

Chapter 5: A Rift in Time

The TARDIS materialized on the edge of a violent rift, its blue exterior standing defiantly against the churning chaos of the multiverse. The surrounding space was a kaleidoscope of broken stars, inverted timelines, and swirling anomalies that flickered in and out of existence. The Doctor stood at the console, staring grimly at the scanner.

"A multiverse rift," the Doctor murmured, running a hand through their hair. "This is bad. Very bad. Space, time, reality—everything's bleeding into everything else. And I bet I know who's responsible."

The TARDIS groaned in agreement as the console lit up with warning signals. The Doctor leaned over, tapping furiously at the controls.

"Let's see... unstable temporal fields, spatial distortions... and oh, what's this?" The Doctor frowned, pointing at a blip on the screen. "A Space Stone. Of course. And if I'm right—and I usually am—there's a shard of the Key to Time in there with it. Brilliant. Just brilliant."

The Doctor flipped a lever, and the TARDIS jolted forward, edging closer to the rift. The energy inside the console room flickered as the vortex outside pushed against the ship.

"Hang on, old girl," the Doctor said, patting the console. "We've got to get in there before—"

Suddenly, a jarring signal interrupted the Doctor's thoughts. A familiar ship appeared on the scanner, sleek and menacing.

"Oh, look who it is," the Doctor muttered, rolling their eyes. "The Master. Can't cause chaos without him showing up, can we?"

On The Master's Ship

The Master stood at his own console, gazing out at the rift with a mixture of awe and triumph. The Space Stone glowed faintly in his hand, its power radiating through the room.

"The multiverse, torn open like a wound," The Master mused, a wicked smile tugging at his lips. "And it's all thanks to me. Well, me and my new favorite toy."

He turned the Stone over in his hand, admiring its brilliance. Nearby, a fragment of the Key to Time hovered within a containment field, pulsing faintly in sync with the Stone. Together, they created a rift that pulsed with raw energy.

"I could do so much with this," The Master murmured, his voice almost reverent. "Rewrite history, reshape the cosmos. But first—"

His ship's console beeped, interrupting his train of thought. He scowled, glancing at the display.

"The Doctor," he said, his voice dripping with disdain. "Always meddling."

The Master activated his communicator, and a holographic screen showed the TARDIS approaching the rift. He smirked.

"Well, Doctor, if you're so eager to join the fun, let's see how you handle this."

He activated the Space Stone, and the rift pulsed violently, sending out a shockwave that struck the TARDIS.

In the TARDIS

The ship shook violently as the shockwave hit, throwing the Doctor off balance. Sparks flew from the console, and the lights flickered dangerously.

"Oh, come on!" the Doctor shouted, pulling themselves up. "That was uncalled for!"

They frantically adjusted controls, stabilizing the TARDIS just as another wave hit.

"Right," the Doctor muttered, narrowing their eyes. "If he wants to play rough, two can play at that game."

With a flick of a switch, the TARDIS surged forward, forcing its way into the rift. The interior of the ship glowed with energy as the Doctor guided it toward the Master's location.

Inside the Rift

The rift was a chaotic nightmare of fragmented realities, with broken pieces of universes colliding and merging in unpredictable ways. The Doctor's TARDIS materialized on a floating platform of cracked stone, barely holding together amidst the storm of energy. A moment later, The Master's ship appeared nearby, sleek and intimidating.

The Doctor stepped out, their expression a mix of frustration and determination. The Master exited his ship with his usual air of smug superiority, the Space Stone glowing faintly in his hand.

"Master," the Doctor said, crossing their arms. "What have you done this time?"

The Master spread his arms dramatically. "Isn't it obvious, Doctor? I've opened a rift in the multiverse. A masterpiece of chaos, if I do say so myself."

"Chaos isn't a masterpiece," the Doctor snapped. "It's a mess. Do you have any idea what you're playing with?"

"Oh, I do," The Master replied, his grin widening. "The Space Stone and a fragment of the Key to Time. Together, they've created this delightful little rift. And soon, I'll have the power to reshape reality itself."

"Or destroy it," the Doctor countered, stepping closer. "This rift is unstable. It's tearing universes apart. If you don't stop—"

"Stop?" The Master interrupted, feigning shock. "Why would I stop? This is exactly what I wanted."

Before the Doctor could respond, the ground beneath them rumbled, and a massive surge of energy erupted from the rift. Out of the chaos emerged a guardian—an enormous, serpentine creature made of swirling energy and fragments of shattered timelines. Its voice boomed like thunder.

"WHO DARES DISTURB THE BALANCE?"

The Doctor and The Master exchanged a look.

"Well," the Doctor said, sighing. "This is new."

The guardian lunged toward them, its form shifting and distorting as it moved. The Master raised the Space Stone, sending out a wave of energy to repel the creature, but it barely flinched.

"Brilliant plan," the Doctor said, dodging another attack. "Got a backup?"

The Master scowled. "This is your fault for showing up."

"My fault?" the Doctor shot back, pulling out their sonic screwdriver. "You're the one who tore a hole in the multiverse!"

The guardian roared, and the platform beneath them began to crack. The Doctor grabbed The Master's arm, pulling him back.

"We have to work together," the Doctor said urgently. "Just this once."

The Master hesitated, his pride warring with his survival instinct. Finally, he nodded. "Fine. But only because I don't fancy being obliterated."

Together, they faced the guardian, their combined efforts barely holding it at bay. The Doctor used the sonic screwdriver to disrupt its energy field, while The Master wielded the Space Stone to stabilize the rift.

"This isn't going to hold," the Doctor shouted. "We need to seal the rift!"

The Master glared at them. "You think I don't know that?"

"Then stop arguing and focus!" the Doctor snapped.

With a final surge of effort, they directed their combined power at the rift. The guardian howled as it was pulled back into the chaos, and the rift began to shrink. The Doctor and The Master staggered back as the platform stabilized.

Breathing heavily, The Master turned to the Doctor. "You're lucky I didn't let you die."

"Likewise," the Doctor replied, dusting themselves off. "But don't think this means we're friends."

The Master smirked. "Wouldn't dream of it."

As The Master retreated to his ship, the Doctor called after him. "You can't keep running, Master! This isn't over."

"Oh, it's only just begun," The Master replied with a grin, vanishing into his ship.

The Doctor sighed, stepping back into the TARDIS. "One disaster down, a multiverse of chaos to go. No pressure."

The TARDIS groaned softly as it dematerialized, leaving the rift behind—a fragile reminder of the delicate balance they were trying to protect.

Chapter 6: The Quantum Nexus

The Quantum Nexus was unlike any other location in the multiverse—a parallel dimension caught in a state of perpetual collapse. Entire landscapes hung in suspended animation, disjointed and fragmented, while the skies churned with chaotic energy. Structures floated upside down, rivers ran backward, and gravity was an unpredictable force. This was a place where reality's rules were not just broken—they were rewritten constantly.

The Master stood in the heart of the Nexus, his black coat billowing as bursts of energy crackled around him. Before him, suspended in a bubble of shifting colors, was the **Reality Stone**, its red surface glowing faintly, intertwined with a shard of the **Key to Time**. The air buzzed with its raw power, distorting everything around it.

He raised his laser screwdriver, scanning the energy field. "Ah, there you are," he said, his voice low and filled with anticipation. "A Stone that doesn't just alter reality—it defines it. And fused with the Key to Time? You're practically begging to be used."

The Master grinned, the possibilities already spinning in his mind. "A multiverse remade in my image. No Doctor, no resistance, no chaos—except, of course, the chaos I allow." He chuckled darkly, stepping closer.

The ground trembled, and the Master stopped abruptly as a massive shard of debris floated past him, crashing into a distant mountain. "Yes, yes, I know," he muttered to himself. "This dimension doesn't like visitors. But I'll be quick."

He raised the laser screwdriver again, tuning its frequency to interact with the energy field. Slowly, the bubble began to dissolve, and the Reality Stone pulsed brighter, as if recognizing its new master.

"Easy does it," the Master whispered, reaching out.

The Doctor Arrives

The TARDIS materialized on the edge of the Nexus, shaking violently as the collapsing dimension fought against the ship's stabilizers. Inside, the Doctor gripped the console, teeth clenched as alarms blared.

"Quantum Nexus," the Doctor muttered, flipping switches and slamming a lever into place. "Of all the collapsing dimensions in all the multiverse, he had to pick this one. The Master and his inferiority complex strike again."

The ship jolted as another ripple tore through the Nexus. Sparks flew from the console, and the Doctor stumbled, catching themselves on the edge of the console. "Oh, come on! Hold together, old girl. We're almost there."

With a final jolt, the TARDIS stabilized, and the Doctor grabbed their coat before stepping outside. The chaotic landscape greeted them, and they immediately spotted the glowing red energy in the distance.

"Well, that's subtle," the Doctor muttered, setting off toward the Reality Stone.

The Confrontation

The Master had just secured the Reality Stone in his hand when the Doctor appeared, stepping over floating debris with practiced ease.

"Master!" the Doctor called out, hands in their pockets, their tone a mixture of exasperation and concern. "What are you doing?"

The Master turned, his grin widening. "Ah, Doctor. You're just in time to witness my ascension. Again."

The Doctor stopped a few feet away, eyeing the Reality Stone. "Do you even know what you're holding? The Reality Stone isn't just some toy. It can—"

"Alter reality itself," the Master interrupted, holding up the glowing red Stone. "Oh, I know exactly what it can do. And I know exactly what I'm going to do with it."

"Let me guess," the Doctor said, crossing their arms. "Rewrite the multiverse to suit your twisted vision? Eliminate anything that doesn't bow to you?"

The Master tilted his head, smirking. "Close. But you make it sound so small-minded. This isn't just about me, Doctor. This is about perfection. Balance. A multiverse without flaws, without conflict."

The Doctor's eyes narrowed. "Without freedom."

The Master chuckled. "Freedom is overrated. Besides, you're hardly one to talk about balance, running around fixing things you don't like."

"That's not the same, and you know it," the Doctor snapped. "You're playing with forces you can't control. The Nexus is already collapsing—if you use that Stone, you'll tear everything apart."

The Master's expression hardened. "Then perhaps it's time for you to see things my way."

Before the Doctor could react, the Master raised the Reality Stone. The world around them warped instantly—trees became metal towers, the ground transformed into reflective glass, and the sky turned a deep crimson. The Doctor stumbled as gravity shifted, pulling them upward.

"Oh, come on!" the Doctor shouted, flailing as they tried to stabilize themselves. They pulled out their sonic screwdriver, scanning the warped environment. "Master, this is ridiculous!"

"Ridiculous?" the Master said, floating effortlessly above the Doctor. "This is artistry, Doctor. My artistry."

The Doctor managed to grab hold of a floating platform, pulling themselves onto it. "Artistry? You've turned the Nexus into a funhouse! How is this helping anyone?"

The Master descended, landing a few feet away. "It's not about helping anyone. It's about proving a point. And right now, the point is that I can trap you in this dimension forever."

The Doctor's eyes widened as the platform they were standing on began to crumble. "Oh, that's just rude!"

They jumped to another platform, narrowly avoiding falling into a chasm of swirling energy. "Master, listen to me. This dimension is unstable. If you keep using that Stone, you'll collapse it completely—and take us both with it."

"Then stop me," the Master challenged, his grin widening. He raised the Reality Stone again, and the Doctor was flung backward as the environment twisted violently.

The Escape

The Doctor clung to the edge of a floating structure, their sonic screwdriver sparking as they adjusted its frequency. "All right, if he wants chaos, let's give him chaos," they muttered.

With a sharp twist, they aimed the sonic at the Reality Stone, sending out a burst of counter-energy. The Master staggered as the Stone pulsed in his hand, momentarily destabilized.

"Doctor!" the Master snarled. "What are you doing?"

"Leveling the playing field," the Doctor called back, scrambling onto solid ground. "You're not the only one who can manipulate reality."

The two faced each other, the Reality Stone glowing fiercely between them. The Doctor's expression was determined, while the Master's was a mix of anger and admiration.

"You can't win, Doctor," the Master said. "This is bigger than you."

"Maybe," the Doctor replied. "But it's not just about winning. It's about doing what's right."

The Master raised the Stone again, but before he could use it, the Doctor activated their sonic screwdriver. A beam of energy struck the Stone, causing it to pulse uncontrollably. The Nexus trembled as the dimension began to collapse further.

"Master, we have to leave!" the Doctor shouted. "The Nexus won't hold much longer!"

The Master hesitated, his grip on the Stone tightening. For a moment, it seemed as though he might refuse. But then he smirked, pocketing the Stone and stepping back.

"Fine," he said. "But this isn't over."

"It never is," the Doctor muttered, running back to the TARDIS.

The Master vanished into his ship as the Nexus imploded behind them, leaving only fragments of its chaotic beauty in its wake.

Aftermath

Inside the TARDIS, the Doctor leaned against the console, catching their breath. "One more Stone... one more disaster." They looked at the scanner, watching as the Master's ship disappeared into the vortex.

"This isn't over," the Doctor whispered, their gaze hardening. "Not by a long shot."

Chapter 7: The Eternal Betrayal

The cavernous chamber deep within the ruins of what had once been the Citadel of Chronos was bathed in an eerie green light. The glow emanated from the **Time Stone**, perched delicately on a pedestal carved from shimmering obsidian. Temporal energy crackled in the air, distorting time itself—seconds stretched into eternities, while minutes folded into fleeting moments.

The Master stood at the edge of the chamber, his dark eyes reflecting the swirling green light of the Time Stone. Beside him were two of his temporary allies, alien mercenaries from a war-torn dimension, their towering, armored forms bristling with weapons. They had proven useful, but their usefulness was nearing an end.

"Well," the Master said, his voice smooth as silk, "here it is. The final piece of our little adventure."

The taller of the two mercenaries, a reptilian being with emerald scales and piercing yellow eyes, stepped forward cautiously. "This artifact... its power is immense. You cannot wield it alone."

The Master smirked, tilting his head. "Oh, I think you'll find that I can."

The second mercenary, shorter but bulkier, let out a low growl. "You promised us a share of the spoils, Time Lord. Betray us, and we'll—"

The Master turned sharply, his grin vanishing as he pointed his laser screwdriver at the mercenary's chest. "You'll do what, exactly? Growl at me some more?"

Before the mercenary could respond, the chamber began to tremble. The glow of the Time Stone intensified, and a faint figure materialized in front of the pedestal. The Master froze, his eyes narrowing as he recognized the figure—it was **himself**, but older, his face lined with time's wear, his expression grim.

"Well, this is awkward," the present Master muttered, striding forward. "Let me guess: you're here to stop me."

The future Master sighed. "No, you idiot. I'm here because I know what happens next. You take the Time Stone. You betray your allies. And then you make a mistake—a critical one."

The present Master raised an eyebrow. "Me? Make a mistake? Hardly."

The future Master took a step closer, his voice low and urgent. "You don't understand the cost of what you're about to do. The Time Stone isn't like the others. It will test you, twist you, and ultimately—"

"Spare me the lecture," the present Master interrupted, rolling his eyes. "You're just jealous that I got here first."

The future Master's expression darkened. "If you take it now, without understanding its power, you'll destroy everything."

The present Master smirked. "That's the point."

Without another word, he activated his laser screwdriver, firing a beam of energy at his future self. The older Master countered with a flick of his wrist, sending a ripple of temporal energy that knocked the present Master backward.

The mercenaries exchanged glances, their weapons drawn. The taller one stepped forward. "What's happening here? You didn't say there'd be—"

"Silence!" both Masters barked in unison.

The present Master regained his footing, his grin returning. "Oh, this is delightful. I always wondered what it'd be like to fight myself."

The future Master's eyes glimmered with regret. "And now you'll find out."

The Doctor Arrives

Outside the chamber, the familiar groan of the TARDIS echoed through the ruins. The Doctor stepped out, their expression a mix of exasperation and determination.

"Time Stone," the Doctor muttered, scanning the area with their sonic screwdriver. "Of course it's the Time Stone. Can't ever pick something simple, can you, Master?"

The Doctor moved cautiously through the ruins, following the green glow. As they neared the chamber, they heard the sound of fighting and the unmistakable voice of the Master—two of them.

"Oh, brilliant," the Doctor muttered, rolling their eyes. "He's arguing with himself. This should be good."

Inside the Chamber

The Masters were locked in a duel of wits and power, each trying to outmaneuver the other with temporal tricks. The mercenaries, caught in the crossfire, were quickly losing patience.

"This is madness," the taller mercenary growled. "We should take the Stone ourselves."

As the mercenary stepped toward the pedestal, the present Master spun around, firing a beam from his screwdriver that sent the alien crashing into the wall.

"Nice try," the present Master said, smirking. "But this is a Time Lord's game."

The Doctor entered the chamber just in time to see the future Master counter with a temporal wave, freezing the present Master in place for a brief moment.

"Oh, this is rich," the Doctor said, stepping forward. "Master versus Master. I should've brought popcorn."

Both Masters turned to face the Doctor, their expressions equally annoyed.

"You," the present Master hissed. "I don't remember inviting you."

The Doctor shrugged. "You never do, but here I am. What's the plan this time? Rewrite history? Collapse the timeline? Or are you just trying to outdo yourself?"

The future Master spoke, his voice cold. "Doctor, you don't understand. If he takes the Time Stone—"

"Oh, I understand perfectly," the Doctor interrupted. "He's about to make a mess of things, as usual. The real question is: why are you trying to stop him?"

The future Master hesitated, his gaze flickering to the Stone. "Because I know what happens if he succeeds."

The Betrayal

As the Doctor and the future Master spoke, the present Master seized his opportunity. With a sly grin, he activated a hidden device on his wrist, releasing a burst of energy that disrupted the temporal field. Both the Doctor and the future Master staggered, momentarily disoriented.

"Thanks for the distraction," the present Master said, striding toward the Time Stone.

The future Master regained his composure just in time to shout, "Stop! You don't know what you're doing!"

"Oh, I think I do," the present Master replied, grabbing the Time Stone. Its energy surged through him, and he laughed maniacally as the power coursed through his veins. "I can see it all—past, present, future. It's beautiful."

The Doctor, still recovering, pointed their sonic screwdriver at the Stone. "Master, let it go! You can't handle that kind of power."

The present Master ignored them, his grin widening as he turned to his future self. "Looks like you were wrong. I'm more than capable."

The future Master's expression darkened. "You've doomed us all."

With a flick of his hand, the present Master activated the Stone's power, creating a temporal bubble that trapped the Doctor and his future self. The bubble began to shrink, its edges glowing with destructive energy.

"Enjoy your little prison," the present Master said, stepping back. "I've got a multiverse to conquer."

The Doctor's Escape

Inside the bubble, the Doctor examined the shrinking walls with frantic determination. "Okay, okay, think. Temporal bubble. Collapsing. Not good."

The future Master glared at them. "This is your fault."

The Doctor shot him a withering look. "Oh, please. You're the one who made this mess in the first place."

Ignoring the bickering, the Doctor adjusted their sonic screwdriver, sending out a pulse that temporarily slowed the bubble's collapse.

"Got it!" the Doctor exclaimed. "If we reverse the polarity of the bubble's temporal field, it should destabilize enough for us to break free."

The future Master raised an eyebrow. "And you think that will work?"

The Doctor grinned. "Do you have a better idea?"

Reluctantly, the future Master used his own device to amplify the Doctor's pulse. The bubble flickered, and with a deafening crack, it shattered, releasing them.

The Doctor turned to the future Master. "You're welcome."

Aftermath

The present Master had already vanished, taking the Time Stone with him. The Doctor sighed, running a hand through their hair.

"Another disaster averted. Barely."

The future Master gave a bitter laugh. "You think this is over? He's only just begun."

The Doctor's gaze hardened. "Then we'll stop him. Together, if we have to."

The future Master hesitated, then nodded. "For now."

As the Doctor returned to the TARDIS, they couldn't shake the feeling that the worst was yet to come. The Master, now armed with the

Time Stone, was more dangerous than ever. And the Doctor knew they would need every ounce of their wit and ingenuity to stop him.

Chapter 8: The Soul's Price

The Soul Stone rested in the center of a vast, obsidian plain beneath a sky of shifting orange and black clouds. At its heart was an ancient altar carved from jagged stone, radiating an aura of sorrow and loss. The air was heavy, not with physical weight, but with emotion—grief, longing, and the faint whisper of voices, as if the very ground mourned its existence.

The Master stepped onto the plain, his usual swagger slightly subdued by the oppressive atmosphere. The glow of the Soul Stone ahead pulled at him, and even he couldn't suppress a shiver as he approached the altar. In his hand, a fragment of the **Key to Time** pulsed faintly, resonating with the Stone's energy.

"Well," he muttered to himself, trying to inject levity into the moment, "this is delightfully ominous."

The closer he got, the louder the whispers became, swirling around him like a storm of voices. He stopped a few feet from the altar, his dark eyes narrowing.

"I know you can hear me," The Master said aloud, his voice cutting through the whispers. "Let's skip the theatrics. I'm here for the Soul Stone. Let's make a deal, shall we?"

The whispers coalesced into a single, deep voice.

"Do you know the price, seeker?"

The Master smirked, brushing his coat aside as he stood tall. "Let me guess—some sort of cryptic, existential toll? Spare me the drama. Name your price, and I'll decide if it's worth paying."

The voice laughed, low and mournful.

"The price is not yours to choose. The Soul Stone demands a sacrifice. A soul for a soul."

The Master's smirk faltered. "A soul for a soul? How quaint." He gestured grandly around him. "And if I don't have one to offer?"

The voice's tone grew darker.

"Then you leave empty-handed. Or you die trying."

The Master chuckled, his grin returning. "Do you have any idea who I am? I don't 'die trying.' I win. Always."

He stepped closer to the altar, his mind racing. The Soul Stone pulsed, its orange light growing brighter as it sensed his approach. He could feel it probing him, reaching into his mind, searching his memories.

"You have taken many lives," the voice said, its tone almost pitying. **"But none that matter to you."**

The Master scoffed. "Oh, that's rich. You think I care about anyone?"

The voice didn't answer, but the Stone's light flared again. Suddenly, images flooded the Master's mind—faces from his past, people he had known, fought, and betrayed.

The Doctor Arrives

The TARDIS materialized on the edge of the plain with its usual groaning hum. The Doctor stepped out cautiously, their face grim as they surveyed the eerie landscape.

"Oh, lovely," the Doctor muttered. "Another cheerful day in the Master's twisted quest for power."

They spotted the Master near the altar, bathed in the Soul Stone's glow. Quickening their pace, the Doctor called out. "Master! Whatever you're doing, stop. You don't know what you're dealing with."

The Master turned, his expression one of annoyance. "Doctor, must you always ruin the moment? Can't I have one existential crisis in peace?"

"Existential crisis?" the Doctor said, raising an eyebrow. "That's new. What's the matter, Master? Stone giving you a hard time?"

The Master gestured toward the altar. "The Soul Stone. It's not like the others. It wants a sacrifice—a soul for a soul. Care to volunteer?"

The Doctor frowned, stepping closer. "You can't be serious. Even you wouldn't—" They stopped, noticing the flicker of doubt in the Master's eyes. "Oh, you would."

"Of course I would," the Master snapped. "But the Stone, in its infinite wisdom, seems to think I care about something—or some-one—enough to make it a proper trade."

The Doctor's face softened. "It's not about just any soul, is it? It's about meaning. Connection."

The Master sneered. "Spare me the lecture on morality, Doctor. I'll find another way."

The Sacrifice

The whispers around the plain intensified as the Master turned back to the altar, his expression darkening. The Soul Stone glowed brighter, and the voice spoke again.

"The choice is yours. A soul for the power you seek."

The Master hesitated. For all his bravado, a shadow of uncertainty crossed his face. His hand tightened around the fragment of the Key to Time, its resonance with the Stone growing stronger.

"You're wasting time," the Doctor said, stepping closer. "Walk away. This isn't worth it."

The Master turned sharply, his expression twisted with anger. "Walk away? You think I've come this far to give up now?"

"Then what's your plan?" the Doctor asked, their voice steady but urgent. "You can't just conjure a sacrifice out of thin air. Unless..."

The Master's silence was all the confirmation they needed.

"No," the Doctor said, their voice dropping. "You can't."

"I can," the Master said, his voice cold. "And I will."

The Soul Stone's light flared, and the whispers grew louder, echoing through the plain. The Master closed his eyes, reaching into the depths of his mind, pulling at the threads of his past. A memory surfaced—one he had buried long ago.

Her face appeared in his mind, a companion from his early years, someone he had trusted before his descent into darkness. Her name was Liora, a brilliant Time Lord who had believed in him once.

The Master opened his eyes, and the Doctor saw the flicker of pain there.

"Master," the Doctor said softly. "You don't have to do this."

The Master didn't respond. He raised his laser screwdriver, and the energy around the altar shifted. The memory of Liora solidified, her form taking shape in the Stone's glow.

"No," the Doctor said, stepping forward. "This isn't you. You're better than this."

"I'm not," the Master said, his voice barely a whisper. "I never was."

With a flick of his wrist, the memory shattered, and the Soul Stone absorbed it. The altar trembled, and the whispers fell silent. The Stone's light dimmed for a moment, then flared with a blinding intensity as it dropped into the Master's hand.

The Doctor stared at him, horror etched on their face. "You didn't just sacrifice a memory. You gave it meaning. You sacrificed your own connection to the past."

The Master turned, the Soul Stone glowing in his palm. "And now, Doctor, I have everything I need."

Aftermath

The Master stepped back from the altar, the Soul Stone radiating power. The Doctor watched him, a mixture of sadness and anger in their eyes.

"You've lost more than you've gained," the Doctor said quietly.

The Master smirked, though it didn't reach his eyes. "Perhaps. But it was worth it."

Without another word, the Master vanished into the void, leaving the Doctor alone in the desolate plain. The TARDIS groaned softly as the Doctor returned, their heart heavy with the knowledge of what the Master had done.

The journey wasn't over, but the Doctor knew one thing for certain—the Master's descent into darkness was complete, and the cost of stopping him would only grow higher.

Chapter 9: The Power of Creation

The Heart of the Universe pulsed in the distance—a swirling nexus of pure energy, the birthplace of stars and galaxies, and the cradle of existence itself. Surrounding it was a maelstrom of chaos, where time and space collided in an endless storm. At the edge of this celestial battleground stood The Master, each of the Stones glowing brightly in his grasp, fused with fragments of the Key to Time.

"This is it," The Master murmured, a dangerous smile playing on his lips as he gazed into the radiant void. "The moment where everything changes. A new reality. My reality."

He raised his hands, and the relics pulsed in unison, sending shockwaves through the fabric of existence. But before he could take the final step, a sound cut through the cacophony—the unmistakable groan of the TARDIS materializing.

The Master turned, his expression twisting into a sneer. "Of course. You couldn't resist, could you, Doctor?"

The TARDIS door creaked open, and the Doctor stepped out, flanked by an eclectic group of allies.

The Doctor's Allies

"Master," the Doctor said, their voice steady but filled with warning. "You've gone too far this time."

"Have I?" The Master replied, spreading his arms. "Or am I finally going far enough?"

The Doctor's companions stepped forward. Among them were:

- **River Song**, her blaster at the ready. "Hello, Sweetie. Miss me?"
- **Jack Harkness**, flashing a roguish grin. "I've faced the end of the universe before, but this? This is something else."
- **Jenny, the Doctor's Daughter**, her determination evident in her stance. "You've messed with the wrong family."

• **K-9**, his mechanical voice chiming in. "Master is a threat. Defensive protocols engaged."

The Doctor smirked, glancing at the group. "You didn't think I'd face you alone, did you, Master?"

The Master chuckled, unimpressed. "A motley crew of has-beens and rejects? Really, Doctor, you should know better. You can't stop me."

The Battle Begins

The Master raised the relics, their power creating a protective barrier around him. The Doctor and their allies sprang into action.

"River, Jack, keep him distracted!" the Doctor shouted. "Jenny, find a way to disrupt that shield!"

River and Jack fired their weapons, the blasts ricocheting off the Master's barrier. The Master raised the Reality Stone, warping the space around them. River dodged as the ground beneath her turned into quicksand, while Jack found himself caught in a temporal loop, repeating the same step over and over.

"Nice try!" Jack shouted, forcing himself free.

Meanwhile, Jenny darted around the battlefield, her keen eyes scanning the Master's barrier. She noticed faint distortions where the energy fluctuated.

"Doctor!" Jenny called. "There's a weak point near the base of the shield!"

The Doctor nodded. "Good work, Jenny! K-9, target that spot!"

"Affirmative, Master," K-9 replied, firing a concentrated energy blast at the weak point. The shield flickered, and the Master staggered slightly.

The Master's expression darkened. "Enough of this!"

He raised the Power Stone, unleashing a wave of raw energy that sent everyone flying. The Doctor rolled to their feet, grimacing.

"Master," the Doctor said, their tone sharper. "This won't end the way you think it will. The Heart of the Universe doesn't obey anyone—not even you."

The Master's grin returned. "That's where you're wrong, Doctor. With the Stones and the Key, I don't need its obedience. I'll remake it in my image."

Turning the Tide

River Song approached the Doctor, her blaster smoking. "We need a plan, Sweetie. This isn't working."

The Doctor's eyes darted around, taking in the battlefield. "The Stones are powering the barrier, but they're also drawing from the Heart itself. If we can disrupt that connection..."

River raised an eyebrow. "You're going to disrupt the Heart of the Universe? Bold move."

"Desperate times," the Doctor said, pulling out their sonic screwdriver.

The Doctor dashed toward the Heart, dodging the Master's attacks. They activated the sonic, sending a pulse toward the Heart's energy stream. The connection wavered, and the Stones flickered.

The Master snarled. "Stop that!"

He raised the Time Stone, freezing the Doctor in place. For a moment, everything stopped—the chaos, the noise, even the flow of time itself.

The Doctor's Gambit

But even frozen, the Doctor's mind raced. They had anticipated this and had set the TARDIS to emit a counter-frequency. The ship activated, breaking the temporal stasis.

"Surprise!" the Doctor shouted, now free.

The Master's frustration boiled over. He raised all the Stones, their combined power creating a vortex of energy. The battlefield trembled as reality itself began to tear apart.

The Doctor's allies regrouped, their determination unshaken.

"River, Jack, Jenny!" the Doctor called. "Focus all your attacks on him. K-9, recalibrate and hit that shield again!"

The combined assault was relentless. River's precision shots, Jack's brute force, Jenny's agility, and K-9's unwavering focus worked in unison. The Master's shield began to crack.

"No!" the Master bellowed, his voice filled with rage. "You can't stop me!"

The Doctor stepped forward, their voice calm but firm. "You've already lost, Master. You always do."

The Final Blow

With one last surge of power, the Master's shield shattered. The Stones flickered wildly, their energy unstable. The Doctor seized the moment, aiming the sonic screwdriver at the relics.

"Let's see how you handle a bit of chaos," the Doctor said, activating the sonic.

The relics emitted a blinding light as the Stones and the fragments of the Key separated, their power dissipating into the Heart of the Universe. The Master screamed, his plans unraveling before his eyes.

"No!" he shouted, collapsing to his knees. "I was so close!"

The Doctor approached him, their expression one of sadness. "You always are. But this isn't the way, Master. It never is."

Aftermath

The Heart of the Universe began to stabilize, its energy calming as the Stones and Key fragments were scattered across the multiverse once more.

River approached the Doctor, holstering her weapon. "Well, that was fun. Let's never do it again."

Jack clapped the Doctor on the shoulder. "You really know how to throw a party."

The Doctor managed a faint smile but turned their attention to the Master. "What happens to him now?"

The Master looked up, his eyes filled with fury. "You think this is over, Doctor? You think I'll stop?"

The Doctor sighed. "No. But for now, the universe is safe."

The TARDIS materialized again, and the Doctor's allies began to board. Before following them, the Doctor glanced back at the Master one last time.

"Goodbye, Master. Until next time."

The Master watched as the TARDIS vanished, his fists clenched. Alone at the edge of the Heart of the Universe, he stared into the void, his mind already plotting his next move.

Chapter 10: The Dark Fulcrum

The void between universes was silent, save for the hum of immense power emanating from the crystalline structure suspended at its center. The **Dark Fulcrum** had been forged—a massive, pulsating construct that combined the energy of the Infinity Stones with the fragments of the Key to Time. It radiated an aura of raw destruction and creation, a paradox that threatened to unmake reality itself.

The Master stood at the base of the Fulcrum, his face illuminated by the chaotic light it emitted. His hands rested on the console he had crafted to control the device, its alien interface pulsing in sync with his heartbeat.

"This," The Master whispered, his voice tinged with awe, "is power. True power." He turned to face the swirling rift beyond. "The multiverse, at my mercy. No more chaos. No more failure. Only order. My order."

He placed his hands on the controls, and the Fulcrum roared to life. A wave of energy shot out, distorting space and time. Entire galaxies flickered in and out of existence as the Fulcrum began rewriting the fabric of reality.

The Doctor Arrives

The TARDIS materialized on the edge of the void, shaking violently as it fought against the energy emanating from the Fulcrum. Inside, the Doctor clung to the console, their expression grim.

"This is worse than I thought," the Doctor muttered, flipping switches and adjusting controls. "He's done it. He's actually done it."

River Song's voice crackled through the comms. "Sweetie, we're barely holding together out here. What's the plan?"

The Doctor frowned. "The plan is… improvise. Get everyone ready. We're going to need every trick in the book for this one."

The TARDIS doors swung open, and the Doctor stepped out onto a platform floating near the Fulcrum. The sight was both mesmerizing and horrifying—a massive, crystalline structure that seemed to pulse with life, its energy warping the space around it.

The Master was waiting, his expression one of smug triumph.

"Ah, Doctor," he said, spreading his arms. "You're just in time to witness the dawn of a new reality."

The Doctor glared at him. "What have you done, Master?"

The Master gestured to the Fulcrum. "I've taken the relics you were so desperate to stop me from collecting and turned them into something extraordinary. The Dark Fulcrum. With it, I can rewrite the multiverse—erase the flaws, the failures, the chaos."

"And destroy countless lives in the process," the Doctor countered. "Do you even hear yourself? This isn't creation. It's annihilation."

The Master's eyes glinted. "Necessary sacrifices, Doctor. You of all people should understand that."

The Confrontation

The Doctor took a step forward, their tone sharp. "You think this is about power? About control? The multiverse isn't something you can shape to your whims, Master. It's alive. It's messy, yes, but it's beautiful because of it."

The Master laughed, the sound cold and bitter. "Spare me your sanctimonious speeches. I've spent my entire life in chaos—betrayed by my people, manipulated by forces beyond comprehension. I will not bow to it any longer."

The Doctor shook their head. "You're not fixing anything. You're breaking it all. And for what? To feed your ego?"

The Master's grin faltered for a moment, replaced by a flicker of doubt. But then he tightened his grip on the controls. "Enough talk. It's time to reshape existence."

He activated the Fulcrum, and a massive shockwave tore through the void. The Doctor stumbled, barely managing to stay upright as the platform beneath them shifted.

The Doctor's Allies

From the TARDIS, River Song, Jack Harkness, Jenny, and K-9 emerged, weapons drawn.

"Doctor," River called out, her blaster aimed at the Fulcrum. "What's the move?"

"Distract him!" the Doctor shouted, pulling out the sonic screwdriver. "I'll try to disable the Fulcrum."

River and Jack opened fire, their shots deflecting off a protective barrier around the Master. Jenny dashed toward the Fulcrum, searching for a weak point, while K-9 provided covering fire.

The Master smirked, raising the Reality Stone to warp the battlefield. The platforms shifted, separating the allies and isolating the Doctor.

"Nice try," The Master taunted. "But you're out of your depth, as always."

The Doctor's Plan

The Doctor worked frantically, using the sonic screwdriver to scan the Fulcrum. The interface was complex, far beyond anything they had encountered before.

"Come on, come on," the Doctor muttered. "There has to be a failsafe. Everything has a failsafe."

The sonic beeped, and the Doctor's eyes lit up. "Gotcha. The Stones are powering the Fulcrum, but the Key fragments are stabilizing it. If I can disrupt the fragments..."

They turned to River, who was pinned behind a floating pillar. "River! I need you to target the base of the Fulcrum! That's where the fragments are anchored."

River nodded, ducking out of cover to fire a precise shot. The blast hit its mark, and one of the fragments shattered. The Fulcrum's glow flickered, and the Master staggered.

"No!" he shouted, his expression twisting with rage. "You won't take this from me!"

The Master's Final Move

Desperate, the Master raised the Time Stone, freezing everyone in place except for himself and the Doctor.

"You always think you're better than me," he snarled, stepping closer to the Doctor. "Always interfering, always meddling. But this time, I win."

The Doctor, frozen but still defiant, managed a faint smile. "Winning isn't destroying everything, Master. It's saving it."

The Master hesitated, the weight of the Doctor's words pressing against his mind. But his resolve hardened. "You'll never understand. Goodbye, Doctor."

He turned back to the Fulcrum, preparing to unleash its full power.

The Doctor's Last Gambit

Unfreezing themselves with a hidden counter-frequency, the Doctor lunged forward, activating the sonic screwdriver. A burst of energy struck the Fulcrum's core, destabilizing it completely.

The Master screamed in frustration as the Fulcrum began to collapse, its energy spiraling out of control.

"You've doomed us both!" he shouted.

The Doctor grabbed the Master by the arm, dragging him away from the imploding structure. "Not if we get out of here now! Move!"

The allies regrouped at the TARDIS, barely escaping as the Fulcrum disintegrated, sending shockwaves through the void.

Aftermath

Inside the TARDIS, the Doctor slumped against the console, exhaustion etched into their features.

River crossed her arms. "That was close. Too close."

Jack grinned. "I've faced worse. Well, maybe not."

The Doctor glanced at the Master, who sat silently in a corner, his expression blank. For once, he had nothing to say.

"This isn't over," the Doctor said softly, more to themselves than anyone else. "Not by a long shot."

The TARDIS hummed, carrying them away from the Heart of the Universe, leaving the remnants of the Dark Fulcrum behind—a testament to the lengths one would go for power and the cost of hubris.

Chapter 11: The Impossible Choice

The void shimmered, unstable and unpredictable. The remnants of the **Dark Fulcrum** hovered ominously, pulsating with chaotic energy. Fractured timelines bled into one another, forming a kaleidoscopic storm where fragments of history and alternate realities collided. Despite its partial destruction, the Fulcrum's core still radiated immense power, and its very presence threatened to unravel the fabric of existence.

The Doctor stood at the edge of the TARDIS platform, staring at the swirling maelstrom. Behind them, their allies—River Song, Jack Harkness, Jenny, and K-9—watched silently. They could feel the weight of the Doctor's internal conflict.

"We can't let this continue," River said, breaking the silence. Her voice was steady but tinged with urgency. "If that thing isn't stopped, it'll tear everything apart."

"I know," the Doctor replied, their voice low. "But stopping it isn't as simple as flipping a switch, River. Destroying the Fulcrum could cause a chain reaction that might... well, unmake everything."

Jack frowned, his usual bravado replaced by concern. "What about the other option? The Master?"

The Doctor turned to face him. "If I try to stop him directly, there's no guarantee I'll succeed. And if he regains control of the Fulcrum, we're back where we started—or worse."

Jenny stepped forward, her eyes fierce. "So what do we do? Just stand here and watch the multiverse fall apart?"

"No," the Doctor said firmly. "We don't just stand here. We think. We plan. We—"

A familiar voice interrupted them, dripping with sarcasm. "Or you can admit defeat and let me handle it."

The Master's Arrival

The Master appeared on a floating shard of debris, his coat billowing in the turbulent winds of the void. Despite the chaos around him, he exuded his usual confidence, though his expression was darker than usual.

"Doctor," he said, his tone mockingly cheerful. "Still trying to save the day, I see. How quaint."

The Doctor glared at him. "You've done enough damage, Master. Walk away while you still can."

The Master laughed, a cold, bitter sound. "Walk away? From this?" He gestured to the Fulcrum. "Do you even understand what I've created? This isn't just destruction, Doctor—it's potential. I could rebuild the multiverse better than it ever was."

"At what cost?" the Doctor snapped. "You've already condemned countless lives. You've torn the timeline to shreds."

The Master stepped closer, his grin fading. "Don't pretend you're any different. You meddle with time just as much as I do. The only difference is, I'm honest about it."

The Dilemma

The Doctor took a step forward, their voice softer now. "You can still stop this, Master. We can find another way."

"There is no other way," the Master said sharply. "The Fulcrum is the answer. And if you won't see that..." He raised his hand, revealing the glowing remnants of the Infinity Stones, still pulsing with energy. "Then I'll make you see."

The Fulcrum roared to life, its energy growing unstable. The void around them trembled, and timelines began to collapse into one another. A Roman centurion flickered into existence beside them before vanishing, replaced by a prehistoric mammoth that let out a confused bellow before it too disappeared.

River stepped forward, her blaster aimed at the Master. "Doctor, we're out of time. We need to act."

The Doctor hesitated, their mind racing. Destroying the Fulcrum outright could cause a catastrophic chain reaction, but confronting the Master directly was equally risky. Both options carried immense consequences, and there was no clear path forward.

"Doctor," Jack said, his voice serious. "You've always been the one to make the impossible choices. What's it going to be?"

The Doctor turned back to the Fulcrum, their face grim. "I need time."

The Master smirked. "Time? That's the one thing you don't have."

The Confrontation

The Doctor stepped closer to the Master, their voice calm but filled with resolve. "You don't have to do this. You've always wanted control, but this isn't control. This is chaos."

The Master's expression darkened. "Don't you dare lecture me about chaos. Do you think I wanted this? Do you think I enjoy being the villain in your story? This was never about power for power's sake, Doctor. This was about proving I could be more."

"You can be more," the Doctor said softly. "But not like this."

For a moment, there was silence. The Master's grip on the Stones faltered, and for the briefest of moments, doubt flickered in his eyes. But then the Fulcrum emitted a violent surge of energy, and the Master's resolve returned.

"No," he said firmly. "This is the only way."

The Doctor's Decision

The Doctor's hands tightened around the sonic screwdriver as they made their choice. "River, Jack, Jenny—get back to the TARDIS. Now."

"What?" River asked, alarmed. "Doctor, you can't—"

"Just go!" the Doctor shouted, their voice cracking with urgency. "I'll handle this."

Reluctantly, the others retreated to the TARDIS. The Doctor turned back to the Master, their face a mix of determination and sadness.

"This is your last chance," the Doctor said. "Stand down, or I will stop you."

The Master laughed bitterly. "You? Stop me? You don't have it in you, Doctor."

The Doctor raised the sonic screwdriver, pointing it at the Fulcrum. "We'll see."

The Climax

The Doctor activated the sonic, sending a focused pulse of energy toward the Fulcrum. The Master reacted instantly, using the Stones to create a shield. The two forces collided, the energy between them crackling violently.

"You can't win!" the Master shouted over the noise. "You'll destroy everything!"

"Better that than let you control it!" the Doctor shot back.

The Fulcrum began to destabilize further, its energy spiraling out of control. The Doctor pushed harder, their face strained with effort. The Master matched them, his expression twisted with determination.

The Breaking Point

The Fulcrum let out a deafening roar as it reached critical mass. The Master staggered, the power slipping from his control. The Doctor saw their chance and redirected the sonic, targeting the Stones themselves.

With a final, blinding explosion, the Fulcrum shattered, its energy dissipating into the void. The Master was thrown backward, landing hard on a floating platform. The Doctor collapsed to their knees, their breath coming in ragged gasps.

Aftermath

The void began to stabilize, the fractured timelines retreating. The Doctor approached the Master, who was still lying on the ground, clutching the broken remnants of the Stones.

"You could've been better," the Doctor said quietly. "You could've been so much more."

The Master looked up at them, his expression a mix of anger and despair. "And you could've stopped me sooner."

The Doctor turned away, their face heavy with regret. "Goodbye, Master."

As the TARDIS dematerialized, the Master was left alone in the void, staring at the ruins of his ambition. His laughter echoed, hollow and broken, as the light of the Fulcrum faded into darkness.

Chapter 12: Shadows and Light

The void surrounding the remnants of the **Dark Fulcrum** had begun to calm, though faint distortions of space and time still rippled across the expanse. The Doctor stood alone on a fragment of rock, staring into the distance where the Fulcrum's energy had dissipated. The silence was unnerving, but it was short-lived.

A familiar voice broke through the stillness, soft and mocking.

"You think it's over, don't you?"

The Doctor turned to see The Master stepping forward from the shadows. His coat was torn, his face marked with burns from the Fulcrum's explosion, but his eyes burned with defiance.

"It doesn't matter what you've destroyed, Doctor," The Master said, his voice low but fierce. "The Key to Time wasn't just a tool. It's alive, sentient, and it has a plan of its own."

The Doctor frowned, gripping their sonic screwdriver tightly. "You're bluffing. The Fulcrum is gone. The Key fragments are scattered across the multiverse again. It's over."

The Master chuckled darkly, reaching into his coat to pull out a small, glowing shard. It pulsed faintly, resonating with an otherworldly hum.

"Is it?" he asked, holding the shard up. "Because this fragment says otherwise. The Key's failsafe is activating, and we're about to find out what happens when its creators designed it to do more than just balance the universe."

The Doctor's eyes widened. "You've triggered it, haven't you? The failsafe."

The Master smirked. "Oh, I didn't just trigger it. I became part of it."

The Key's Awakening

Before the Doctor could respond, the shard in the Master's hand flared to life, and a bright light engulfed the void. Both Time Lords shielded their eyes as the shards of the Key to Time, scattered across the multiverse, began to coalesce. Streams of energy surged from every direction, converging into a single point—a glowing, crystalline sphere that hovered above them, pulsing with infinite power.

The Doctor stared in awe. "The Key... it's reforming itself. But how?"

The Master stepped forward, his voice filled with triumph. "Because it's tired of being used, Doctor. Tired of serving as a pawn in a game it didn't ask to play. The Time Lords thought they could control it, but they underestimated its purpose."

The crystalline sphere pulsed, and a deep, resonant voice echoed through the void—a voice that seemed to come from everywhere and nowhere at once.

"I am the Key to Time. I am the balance, the creation, the destruction. And I have awakened."

The Doctor stepped back, their expression a mixture of fear and determination. "You don't have to do this," they said, addressing the Key. "The multiverse is already fragile enough. Let us fix it. We can restore balance without—"

"SILENCE," the Key commanded, its voice shaking the void. **"Balance has been broken. Interference from the Time Lords and others has left the multiverse in disarray. I must recalibrate existence."**

The Doctor exchanged a glance with the Master, who, for the first time, looked genuinely uncertain. "Recalibrate?" the Master asked, his voice tinged with hesitation. "What does that mean?"

The Key pulsed again, its light growing brighter.

"The multiverse will be reset. All anomalies erased. All interference undone. A new beginning."

The Impossible Alliance

The Doctor stepped forward, their voice urgent. "Wait! You can't just reset everything. Do you have any idea what that means? Lives will be lost—entire realities wiped out."

The Key's voice remained impassive. **"A sacrifice for balance."**

The Master's expression darkened. "You think I'll let you erase me? I've fought too hard, too long, to be rewritten by some glorified cosmic artifact."

The Doctor turned to him, their voice sharp. "This is your fault, Master. You unleashed the Key's failsafe, and now it's out of control."

The Master scowled. "Don't you dare blame me. You're the one who destroyed the Fulcrum. This is as much your doing as it is mine."

The Key's energy surged, and the ground beneath them began to fragment.

"The reset will begin."

The Doctor turned to the Master, their expression resolute. "We have to stop it."

"And how do you propose we do that, genius?" the Master snapped.

"Together," the Doctor said simply.

The Master blinked, momentarily stunned by the suggestion. "You're serious."

"Deadly serious," the Doctor replied. "We can't let it reset the multiverse. Not like this. But I can't do it alone."

The Master hesitated, the conflict clear in his eyes. Finally, he nodded, a reluctant smile tugging at his lips. "Fine. But if we survive this, I want it on record that I saved the multiverse."

The Final Confrontation

The Doctor and the Master approached the Key, their combined energy shielding them from its immense power.

"Key!" the Doctor called out, their voice firm. "Listen to me. The multiverse doesn't need a reset. It needs a chance. Let us help you restore balance without destroying everything."

The Key's voice boomed. **"You speak of chances, yet your kind has squandered them time and again."**

The Master stepped forward, his tone sly. "Oh, come now. Even gods can make mistakes. Surely you're not so perfect that you can't admit that?"

The Key's light dimmed slightly, as if considering his words.

The Doctor seized the moment. "You were created to preserve balance, not destroy it. Resetting the multiverse would only repeat the cycle of chaos. Let us show you another way."

The Key hesitated, its energy fluctuating. **"What way?"**

The Doctor exchanged a glance with the Master, then stepped closer. "Disperse your energy. Return to the fabric of the multiverse. Let existence heal itself naturally."

The Master smirked. "What the Doctor means is: trust us. We're brilliant."

The Twist

The Key pulsed one last time, its voice softening. **"Very well. But know this, Doctor. The balance you seek to restore will come at a cost."**

The Doctor frowned. "What cost?"

Before the Key could answer, its energy surged outward, enveloping the Doctor and the Master. Memories, timelines, and possibilities flooded their minds. When the light faded, the Key was gone, its energy dispersed across the multiverse.

The void was silent once more.

Aftermath

The Doctor and the Master stood in the stillness, both visibly shaken.

"Well," the Master said, breaking the silence. "That was... anticlimactic."

The Doctor shot him a look. "Anticlimactic? The multiverse was nearly destroyed, and you think that was anticlimactic?"

The Master shrugged, his grin returning. "Admit it, Doctor. You couldn't have done it without me."

The Doctor sighed, turning toward the TARDIS. "Maybe. But don't think this changes anything."

"Oh, I wouldn't dream of it," the Master said, his tone playful.

As the Doctor entered the TARDIS, they paused, looking back at the Master. "You could come with me, you know. Be better."

The Master's smile faded slightly. "Tempting. But no. I've got my own path to follow."

The Doctor nodded, their expression sad but understanding. "Until next time."

"Until next time," the Master echoed, watching as the TARDIS dematerialized.

Alone in the void, the Master stared into the distance, his mind already plotting his next move. Despite everything, he couldn't help but smile. The game wasn't over—not by a long shot.

Epilogue: A Universe Reborn

The TARDIS floated silently in the cosmic expanse, a lone blue box against the shimmering backdrop of the reborn multiverse. The Doctor sat slouched against the console, their face a canvas of exhaustion and quiet contemplation. Around them, the TARDIS hummed gently, as if sensing its pilot's weariness.

The multiverse had survived—but just barely.

The Doctor stood, pacing around the console, their mind racing with the enormity of what had happened. Fractured timelines had re-aligned, universes stitched themselves back together, and the chaotic echoes of the **Dark Fulcrum** were fading into distant memory. Yet the multiverse didn't feel the same.

"It's... different," the Doctor murmured to themselves. "Not broken, but... changed."

The TARDIS responded with a low groan, and the Doctor nodded. "I know. It's not just me, is it? Something's shifted."

They reached for a lever but hesitated, their hand lingering in the air. Memories of the **Key to Time**'s final words echoed in their mind: **"The balance you seek to restore will come at a cost."**

"What cost?" the Doctor whispered, their voice barely audible.

Revisiting the Consequences

A holographic projection flickered into view above the console, displaying a map of the multiverse. The once-chaotic rifts had smoothed into intricate patterns, like the weaving of an impossibly complex tapestry. The Doctor traced a finger along one of the threads, frowning.

"Worlds I've visited... but they're not quite the same. People... events... all slightly altered."

The Doctor's brow furrowed deeper as they tapped the console, pulling up specific timelines. One showed a version of Earth where humanity had discovered advanced technology a century earlier. Another displayed a Gallifrey that had never fallen to war.

"Recalibration," the Doctor muttered. "The Key wasn't just restoring balance—it was rewriting it."

For all their victories, the Doctor couldn't help but feel the weight of what had been lost. Small, precious moments that no longer existed, people who might have been rewritten out of existence. But the multiverse was stable. For now.

A Familiar Shadow

The TARDIS jolted suddenly, its lights dimming as the central console pulsed erratically. The Doctor braced themselves, frowning as the scanner flared to life.

"What now?" the Doctor muttered, tapping the console. The screen displayed a faint signal—a ripple of energy emanating from the edge of a distant galaxy.

The Doctor's eyes narrowed. The signal was unmistakable. "Oh, no. You can't be serious."

They adjusted the controls, zooming in on the signal. It was faint but growing stronger, and its signature was all too familiar.

The Master.

The Master's New Game

Far from the TARDIS, on a desolate world shrouded in darkness, the Master stood atop a crumbling tower. His coat was ragged, his face etched with a mix of triumph and bitterness. The remains of the **Infinity Stones** and fragments of the **Key to Time** lay scattered on a makeshift altar before him. Though the artifacts were shattered, their residual energy lingered—a testament to their immense power.

He reached down, picking up a fragment of the Key. It glowed faintly in his hand, and he smirked.

"They think it's over," he said to the empty air, his voice laced with venom. "They think the multiverse is safe."

The fragment pulsed in response, as if agreeing with him.

"They're wrong," the Master continued, his tone softening into something almost reverent. "This isn't the end. It's the beginning."

He turned, gazing out at the swirling void beyond the crumbling tower. "The Key may be scattered, but its memory lingers. And memories... can be powerful things."

The Doctor's Resolve

Back in the TARDIS, the Doctor leaned against the console, their eyes fixed on the scanner.

"Master," they murmured, a mixture of frustration and sadness in their voice. "You never know when to stop, do you?"

The Doctor straightened, flipping a series of switches and pulling a lever. The TARDIS groaned in protest, but its engines roared to life, hurtling toward the source of the signal.

"Whatever you're planning, I won't let you win," the Doctor said, their voice steady with resolve. "Not this time. Not ever."

A Universe Watching

As the TARDIS disappeared into the vortex, the camera panned out across the reborn multiverse. Stars burned brighter, new worlds formed, and timelines intertwined in complex, delicate harmony. But beneath the surface, faint ripples hinted at unseen forces still in play.

The multiverse was stable, but its balance was precarious. The Key to Time's recalibration had created something new—something unpredictable. And somewhere, in the depths of the void, ancient powers stirred, watching, waiting.

A Tease for the Future

The Master, still holding the fragment of the Key, turned back to his altar. He placed the shard carefully in the center, surrounding it with remnants of the Stones. His grin widened as the fragment began to glow brighter, its light casting long, ominous shadows.

"Oh, Doctor," he whispered, his tone dripping with malice. "You've only delayed the inevitable. Next time, you won't stop me."

As the light grew, the scene faded to black, leaving only the Master's laughter echoing in the darkness.

The multiverse had been reborn, but its future was anything but certain. And for the Doctor and the Master, the game was far from over.

Appendix A: The Relics of Infinity and Time

The multiverse is shaped by forces beyond comprehension—primordial artifacts imbued with powers that defy the laws of physics, time, and reality itself. Among these are the **Infinity Stones** and the **Key to Time**, each a relic of unimaginable potential, born from vastly different origins yet connected through their shared ability to shape existence. When fused, they form a power so immense that even the most ancient beings fear its consequences.

The Infinity Stones

The Infinity Stones are six singularities, remnants of the multiverse's creation. Each Stone governs a fundamental aspect of existence. Though small in size, their power is limitless, requiring a wielder of immense strength—or cunning—to control them without succumbing to their might.

1. Mind Stone

- **Origin:** A fragment of sentient energy from the moment consciousness emerged in the universe.
- **Abilities:** Grants the wielder unparalleled control over minds, allowing telepathy, mind manipulation, and the power to create sentient beings. It can enhance intelligence or extract hidden knowledge from others.
- **Significance in the Fulcrum:** When fused with the Key to Time, it became the central hub of decision-making within the Dark Fulcrum, amplifying its strategic and analytical capabilities.

2. Space Stone

- **Origin:** Formed at the birth of spatial dimensions, embodying the vastness of the cosmos.
- **Abilities:** Grants the ability to manipulate space, enabling teleportation, wormhole creation, and spatial distortions. It can bend reality to bring distant objects into reach.

- **Significance in the Fulcrum:** Integrated with the Key, it allowed the Fulcrum to reshape the spatial fabric of the multiverse, bending galaxies and dimensions to its will.

3. Reality Stone

- **Origin:** A fragment of the primal energy that formed the first elements of the universe.
- **Abilities:** Alters the fabric of reality, making the impossible possible. It can rewrite the laws of physics and change the nature of existence itself.
- **Significance in the Fulcrum:** When fused, it provided the Fulcrum with its most dangerous power—the ability to rewrite the multiverse on a fundamental level.

4. Power Stone

- **Origin:** Formed from the raw energy of the first exploding stars.
- **Abilities:** Amplifies strength, durability, and energy projection to cosmic levels. It can destroy entire planets with a single strike.
- **Significance in the Fulcrum:** Enhanced the Fulcrum's energy output, making it capable of releasing destructive waves across multiple dimensions.

5. Time Stone

- **Origin:** A fragment of the first time loop, born when linear progression gave way to cycles of cause and effect.
- **Abilities:** Controls the flow of time, enabling time travel, temporal loops, and the ability to accelerate or reverse events.
- **Significance in the Fulcrum:** Allowed the Fulcrum to stabilize its existence across all timelines, effectively rendering it eternal and unchangeable.

6. Soul Stone

- **Origin:** The essence of life itself, formed when the first beings gained self-awareness and emotion.
- **Abilities:** Governs the realm of the soul, granting the ability to manipulate life, death, and the spiritual plane. It demands a sacrifice, a soul for a soul, binding it to the wielder's very essence.
- **Significance in the Fulcrum:** Infused the Fulcrum with the ability to assess and determine the "worthiness" of entire realities, deciding their survival or destruction.

The Key to Time

The Key to Time is an artifact of ancient design, created by the **Guardians of Time** to maintain balance across the multiverse. Unlike the Infinity Stones, which are elemental forces, the Key is an intricate mechanism, divided into six fragments. Each fragment contains a piece of the multiverse's governing framework, and when assembled, the Key becomes a tool capable of unimaginable precision.

Origin of the Key

The Key was forged at the dawn of the multiverse by beings who understood the chaos inherent in unbridled creation. It was designed to recalibrate existence, restore balance, and prevent anomalies from spiraling out of control. The Guardians of Time entrusted its fragments to different dimensions, ensuring that no single being could wield its full power unchecked.

Abilities of the Key

- **Temporal Precision:** The Key can align timelines, correct paradoxes, and stabilize collapsing dimensions.
- **Existence Manipulation:** It allows the recalibration of reality itself, undoing anomalies and reweaving the threads of existence.
- **Sentience:** The Key possesses a rudimentary consciousness, allowing it to evaluate the intentions of its wielder. This sentience is the failsafe against misuse but can also lead to unpredictable consequences.

The Fusion of the Relics

The fusion of the Infinity Stones and the Key to Time occurred when The Master harnessed their combined power to create the **Dark Fulcrum**, a weapon capable of rewriting the multiverse. This fusion was not a simple combination of abilities—it was an unprecedented synergy that amplified both artifacts beyond their original design.

Unified Abilities

- **Omniversal Control:** The Fulcrum allowed its wielder to manipulate not just individual universes but the entire multiverse, reshaping it as they saw fit.
- **Creation and Destruction:** The fusion balanced the Infinity Stones' raw power with the Key's precision, enabling the user to destroy realities or craft new ones from scratch.
- **Sentient Intent:** The Key's consciousness merged with the Stones' energies, creating an entity with its own goals: balance at any cost.

Consequences of the Fusion

The fusion destabilized the multiverse, leading to catastrophic anomalies and near-total collapse. The Key's failsafe was triggered, forcing a recalibration that altered the course of history across countless realities. Though the Dark Fulcrum was destroyed, the ripple effects of its power linger, and the multiverse remains forever changed.

Legacy of the Relics

Both the Infinity Stones and the Key to Time are now scattered once more, their fragments hidden across the reborn multiverse. Their power remains a lingering threat, and their influence can still be felt in subtle ways.

- **For the Doctor:** The relics serve as a reminder of the fragile balance they fight to protect and the dangers of unchecked ambition.
- **For the Master:** They are a symbol of unfinished potential, a source of obsession that continues to drive his schemes.

The story of the Infinity Stones and the Key to Time is far from over. As long as their fragments exist, so too does the possibility of their reunion—and the danger it brings.

This appendix concludes with the following cautionary note:

The multiverse, though stable for now, is a delicate web. Any attempt to manipulate its core artifacts may bring unforeseen consequences, reminding all who seek control that ultimate power is always fleeting.

Appendix B: The Master's Manifesto

The following excerpt is taken from what has come to be known as **The Master's Manifesto**, a chilling document discovered in the aftermath of the Dark Fulcrum's collapse. The writings were encoded within the remnants of the Fulcrum's core, scattered across the multiverse. Scholars of temporal and cosmic history have pieced together fragments of this text, which offers a haunting glimpse into The Master's ultimate vision for the multiverse.

"The Fabric of Weakness"

The multiverse is a lie.

It parades itself as infinite, vast, and immutable, a collection of endless possibilities and untold wonders. But beneath its shimmering surface lies weakness—a fragile web of contradictions, failures, and wasted potential. The multiverse is not a testament to creation's brilliance but a glaring reminder of its inefficiency.

I have traveled through its cracks, danced between its worlds, and unraveled its secrets. I have seen the same patterns repeated over and over: civilizations rising and falling, lives ending in futility, chaos masquerading as freedom. The multiverse is not a masterpiece—it is a mistake.

And I intend to fix it.

"On the Doctor"

You might ask, "Why do you fight the Doctor? Why not join forces and work together for a greater good?"

To that, I say: the Doctor is the multiverse's greatest enabler.

The Doctor perpetuates this broken system, patching its wounds with well-meaning but temporary solutions. They cling to ideals of hope, compassion, and freedom, failing to see that these are the very tools of entropy. Their interventions, while noble on the surface, only delay the inevitable collapse of a multiverse unfit to exist.

But the Doctor is also my mirror. They show me what I might have been, had I allowed myself to be shackled by sentimentality. And that is why I will never stop opposing them—not out of hatred, but out of necessity. The multiverse cannot have two architects, and I will not bow to their inferior vision.

"The True Purpose of the Dark Fulcrum"

The Dark Fulcrum was not a weapon. It was a scalpel, designed to excise the cancer of chaos from the multiverse. The Infinity Stones provided the raw power, while the Key to Time offered the precision needed to rewrite existence. Together, they formed the perfect instrument for creation.

I never sought to destroy the multiverse. I sought to perfect it. To erase its flaws and rebuild it in my image—a multiverse of order, symmetry, and purpose. Imagine a reality without war, without famine, without the aimless wandering of species destined to destroy themselves.

I could have made that reality. I still can.

The Doctor calls me a tyrant. Perhaps I am. But a tyrant with vision is better than a shepherd of mediocrity.

"The Cost of Balance"

Many fear the cost of my vision. They ask, "What will you sacrifice to achieve this utopia?"

The answer is simple: whatever it takes.

Freedom is overrated. It breeds anarchy, undermines progress, and allows the weak to dictate the fate of the strong. Balance demands sacrifice—not just of individuals, but of entire timelines, entire realities. A gardener does not weep for the weeds they pull; they understand that the health of the garden depends on their removal.

I am the gardener of the multiverse. And my shears are sharp.

"My Legacy"

The Doctor believes in moments, in small victories, in fleeting acts of kindness that ripple through time. I believe in permanence.

My legacy will not be written in the stars but in the very fabric of reality itself. When I am finished, there will be no need for a Doctor, no need for heroes or villains. There will only be order—a multiverse that functions as it should, free from the chaos that has plagued it for eternity.

They will curse my name, but they will thank me in the end. Because what I offer is not just power, not just vision. I offer salvation.

"To Those Who Would Resist"

You may fight me. You may rail against my methods, call me a monster, a tyrant, a madman. I have heard it all before, and it has never stopped me.

Do you not see? Your resistance is proof of the multiverse's sickness. You cling to your flawed realities, unwilling to see the grand design I offer. But no matter. You will either bow to my vision or become fuel for it.

The multiverse does not need your consent to be perfected.

"The Final Word"

The Doctor believes the game is over. They are wrong. The Fulcrum may be gone, but its memory remains, its potential etched into the fabric of the multiverse.

I will return—not as a villain, not as a rival, but as the architect of a new era. When I stand at the center of my creation, reshaping existence with the same precision and power I have always sought, they will finally understand.

The multiverse will kneel. And it will be glorious.

Analysis of the Manifesto

Scholars and historians have debated the implications of The Master's Manifesto since its discovery. Some view it as the ramblings of a megalomaniac, while others see it as a chillingly rational critique of the multiverse's flaws. The Doctor, for their part, has refused to comment on the document, save for one cryptic remark:

"Perhaps the scariest thing about the Master's words is that, in some twisted way, they're not entirely wrong. But the difference between us will always be how we choose to act on what we see."

The Master's legacy, as detailed in this manifesto, serves as both a warning and a challenge. Whether his vision will ever come to pass remains uncertain, but one thing is clear: his story is far from over.

This appendix concludes with the following observation:

The Master's Manifesto is more than a declaration of intent—it is a reflection of the multiverse's darkest potential, a stark reminder of the thin line between order and tyranny.

<u>Message from the Author:</u>

I hope you enjoyed this book, I love astrology and knew there was not a book such as this out on the shelf. I love metaphysical items as well. Please check out my other books:

-Life of Government Benefits

-My life of Hell

-My life with Hydrocephalus

-Red Sky

-World Domination:Woman's rule

-World Domination:Woman's Rule 2: The War

-Life and Banishment of Apophis: book 1

-The Kidney Friendly Diet

-The Ultimate Hemp Cookbook

-Creating a Dispensary(legally)

-Cleanliness throughout life: the importance of showering from childhood to adulthood.

-Strong Roots: The Risks of Overcoddling children

-Hemp Horoscopes: Cosmic Insights and Earthly Healing

- Celestial Hemp Navigating the Zodiac: Through the Green Cosmos

-Astrological Hemp: Aligning The Stars with Earth's Ancient Herb

-The Astrological Guide to Hemp: Stars, Signs, and Sacred Leaves

-Green Growth: Innovative Marketing Strategies for your Hemp Products and Dispensary

-Cosmic Cannabis

-Astrological Munchies

-Henry The Hemp

-Zodiacal Roots: The Astrological Soul Of Hemp

- Green Constellations: Intersection of Hemp and Zodiac

-Hemp in The Houses: An astrological Adventure Through The Cannabis Galaxy

-Galactic Ganja Guide

Heavenly Hemp

Zodiac Leaves

Doctor Who Astrology

Cannastrology

Stellar Satvias and Cosmic Indicas

<u>Celestial Cannabis: A Zodiac Journey</u>

AstroHerbology: The Sky and The Soil: Volume 1

AstroHerbology:Celestial Cannabis:Volume 2

Cosmic Cannabis Cultivation

The Starry Guide to Herbal Harmony: Volume 1

The Starry Guide to Herbal Harmony: Cannabis Universe: Volume 2

Yugioh Astrology: Astrological Guide to Deck, Duels and more

Nightmare Mansion: Echoes of The Abyss

Nightmare Mansion 2: Legacy of Shadows

Nightmare Mansion 3: Shadows of the Forgotten

Nightmare Mansion 4: Echoes of the Damned

The Life and Banishment of Apophis: Book 2

Nightmare Mansion: Halls of Despair

<u>Healing with Herb: Cannabis and Hydrocephalus</u>

<u>Planetary Pot: Aligning with Astrological Herbs: Volume 1</u>

Fast Track to Freedom: 30 Days to Financial Independence Using AI, Assets, and Agile Hustles

<u>Cosmic Hemp Pathways</u>

How to Become Financially Free in 30 Days: 10,000 Paths to Prosperity

Zodiacal Herbage: Astrological Insights: Volume 1

Nightmare Mansion: Whispers in the Walls
The Daleks Invade Atlantis
Henry the hemp and Hydrocephalus

10X The Kidney Friendly Diet
Cannabis Universe: Adult coloring book
Hemp Astrology: The Healing Power of the Stars
Zodiacal Herbage: Astrological Insights: Cannabis Universe: Volume 2
<u>**Planetary Pot: Aligning with Astrological Herbs: Cannabis Universes: Volume 2**</u>
Doctor Who Meets the Replicators and SG-1: The Ultimate Battle for Survival
Nightmare Mansion: Curse of the Blood Moon
<u>**The Celestial Stoner: A Guide to the Zodiac**</u>
Cosmic Pleasures: Sex Toy Astrology for Every Sign
Hydrocephalus Astrology: Navigating the Stars and Healing Waters
Lapis and the Mischievous Chocolate Bar

Celestial Positions: Sexual Astrology for Every Sign
Apophis's Shadow Work Journal: : A Journey of Self-Discovery and Healing
Kinky Cosmos: Sexual Kink Astrology for Every Sign
Digital Cosmos: The Astrological Digimon Compendium
Stellar Seeds: The Cosmic Guide to Growing with Astrology
Apophis's Daily Gratitude Journal

Cat Astrology: Feline Mysteries of the Cosmos
The Cosmic Kama Sutra: An Astrological Guide to Sexual Positions
Unleash Your Potential: A Guided Journal Powered by AI Insights
Whispers of the Enchanted Grove

Cosmic Pleasures: An Astrological Guide to Sexual Kinks

369, 12 Manifestation Journal

Whisper of the nocturne journal(blank journal for writing or drawing)

The Boogey Book

Locked In Reflection: A Chastity Journey Through Locktober

Generating Wealth Quickly:

How to Generate $100,000 in 24 Hours

Star Magic: Harness the Power of the Universe

The Flatulence Chronicles: A Fart Journal for Self-Discovery

The Doctor and The Death Moth

Seize the Day: A Personal Seizure Tracking Journal

The Ultimate Boogeyman Safari: A Journey into the Boogie World and Beyond

Whispers of Samhain: 1,000 Spells of Love, Luck, and Lunar Magic: Samhain Spell Book

Apophis's guides:

Witch's Spellbook Crafting Guide for Halloween

<u>Frost & Flame: The Enchanted Yule Grimoire of 1000 Winter Spells</u>

<u>The Ultimate Boogey Goo Guide & Spooky Activities for Halloween Fun</u>

Harmony of the Scales: A Libra's Spellcraft for Balance and Beauty

The Enchanted Advent: 36 Days of Christmas Wonders

Nightmare Mansion: The Labyrinth of Screams

Harvest of Enchantment: 1,000 Spells of Gratitude, Love, and Fortune for Thanksgiving

The Boogey Chronicles: A Journal of Nightly Encounters and Shadowy Secrets

The 12 Days of Financial Freedom: A Step-by-Step Christmas Countdown to Transform Your Finances

Sigil of the Eternal Spiral Blank Journal

A Christmas Feast: Timeless Recipes for Every Meal

Holiday Stress-Free Solutions: A Survival Guide to Thriving During the Festive Season

Yu-Gi-Oh! Holiday Gifting Mastery: The Ultimate Guide for Fans and Newcomers Alike

Holiday Harmony: A Hydrocephalus Survival Guide for the Festive Season

Celestial Craft: The Witch's Almanac for 2025 – A Cosmic Guide to Manifestations, Moons, and Mystical Events

Doctor Who: The Toymaker's Winter Wonderland

Tulsa King Unveiled: A Thrilling Guide to Stallone's Mafia Masterpiece

Pendulum Craft: A Complete Guide to Crafting and Using Personalized Divination Tools

Nightmare Mansion: Santa's Eternal Eve

Starlight Noel: A Cosmic Journey through Christmas Mysteries

The Dark Architect: Unlocking the Blueprint of Existence

Surviving the Embrace: The Ultimate Guide to Encounters with The Hugging Molly

The Enchanted Codex: Secrets of the Craft for Witches, Wiccans, and Pagans

Harvest of Gratitude: A Complete Thanksgiving Guide

Yuletide Essentials: A Complete Guide to an Authentic and Magical Christmas

Celestial Smokes: A Cosmic Guide to Cigars and Astrology

Living in Balance: A Comprehensive Survival Guide to Thriving with Diabetes Insipidus

Cosmic Symbiosis: The Venom Zodiac Chronicles

The Cursed Paw of Ambition

Cosmic Symbiosis: The Astrological Venom Journal

Celestial Wonders Unfold: A Stargazer's Guide to the Cosmos (2024-2029)

The Ultimate Black Friday Prepper's Guide: Mastering Shopping Strategies and Savings

Cosmic Sales: The Astrological Guide to Black Friday Shopping

Legends of the Corn Mother and Other Harvest Myths

Whispers of the Harvest: The Corn Mother's Journal

The Evergreen Spellbook

The Doctor Meets the Boogeyman

The White Witch of Rose Hall's SpellBook

The Gingerbread Golem's Shadow: A Study in Sweet Darkness

The Gingerbread Golem Codex: An Academic Exploration of Sweet Myths

The Gingerbread Golem Grimoire: Sweet Magicks and Spells for the Festive Witch

The Curse of the Gingerbread Golem

10-minute Christmas Crafts for kids

<u>Christmas Crisis Solutions: The Ultimate Last-Minute Survival Guide</u>

Gingerbread Golem Recipes: Holiday Treats with a Magical Twist

The Infinite Key: Unlocking Mystical Secrets of the Ages

Enchanted Yule: A Wiccan and Pagan Guide to a Magical and Memorable Season

Dinosaurs of Power: Unlocking Ancient Magick

Astro-Dinos: The Cosmic Guide to Prehistoric Wisdom

Gallifrey's Yule Logs: A Festive Doctor Who Cookbook

The Dino Grimoire: Secrets of Prehistoric Magick

The Gift They Never Knew They Needed

The Gingerbread Golem's Culinary Alchemy: Enchanting Recipes for a Sweetly Dark Feast

A Time Lord Christmas: Holiday Adventures with the Doctor

Krampusproofing Your Home: Defensive Strategies for Yule

Silent Frights: A Collection of Christmas Creepypastas to Chill Your Bones

Santa Raptor's Jolly Carnage: A Dino-Claus Christmas Tale

Prehistoric Palettes: A Dino Wicca Coloring Journey

The Christmas Wishkeeper Chronicles

The Starlight Sleigh: A Holiday Journey

Elf Secrets: The True Magic of the North Pole

Candy Cane Conjurations

Cooking with Kids: Recipes Under 20 Minutes

Doctor Who: The TARDIS Confiscation

The Anxiety First Aid Kit: Quick Tools to Calm Your Mind

Frosty Whispers: A Winter's Tale

The Infinite Key: Unlocking the Secrets to Prosperity, Resilience, and Purpose

The Grasping Void: Why You'll Regret This Purchase

Astrology for Busy Bees: Star Signs Simplified

The Instant Focus Formula: Cut Through the Noise

The Secret Language of Colors: Unlocking the Emotional Codes

Sacred Fossil Chronicles: Blank Journal

The Christmas Cottage Miracle

Feeding Frenzy: Graboid-Inspired Recipes

Manifest in Minutes: The Quick Law of Attraction Guide

The Symbiote Chronicles: Doctor Who's Venomous Journey

Think Tiny, Grow Big: The Minimalist Mindset

The Energy Key: Unlocking Limitless Motivation

New Year, New Magic: Manifesting Your Best Year Yet

Unstoppable You: Mastering Confidence in Minutes

Infinite Energy: The Secret to Never Feeling Drained

Lightning Focus: Mastering the Art of Productivity in a Distracted World

Saturnalia Manifestation Magick: A Guide to Unlocking Abundance During the Solstice

Graboids and Garland: The Ultimate Tremors-Themed Christmas Guide

12 Nights of Holiday Magic

The Power of Pause: 60-Second Mindfulness Practices

The Quick Reset: How to Reclaim Your Life After Burnout

The Shadow Eater: A Tale of Despair and Survival

The Micro-Mastery Method: Transform Your Skills in Just Minutes a Day

Reclaiming Time: How to Live More by Doing Less

Chronovore: The Eternal Nexus

The Mind Reset: Unlocking Your Inner Peace in a Chaotic World

Confidence Code: Building Unshakable Self-Belief

Baby the Vampire Terrier

Baby the Vampire Terrier's Christmas Adventure

Celestial Streams: The Content Creator's Astrology Manual

The Wealth Whisperer: Unlocking Abundance with Everyday Actions

The Energy Equation: Maximize Your Output Without Burning Out

The Happiness Algorithm: Science-Backed Steps to Joyful Living

Stress-Free Success: Achieving Goals Without Anxiety

Mindful Wealth: The New Blueprint for Financial Freedom

The Festive Flavors of New Year: A Culinary Celebration

If you want solar for your home go here: https://www.harborso-lar.live/apophisenterprises/

Get Some Tarot cards: https://www.makeplayingcards.com/sell/apophis-occult-shop

<u>Get some shirts: https://www.bonfire.com/store/apophis-shirt-emporium/</u>

<u>Instagrams:</u>
@apophis_enterprises,
@apophisbookemporium,
@apophisscardshop
Twitter: @apophisenterpr1
Tiktok:@apophisenterprise
Youtube: @sg1fan23477, @FiresideRetreatKingdom
Hive: @sg1fan23477
CheeLee: @SG1fan23477

Podcast: Apophis Chat Zone: https://open.spotify.com/show/5zXbrCLEV2xzCp8ybrfHsk?si=fb4d4fdbdce44dec

Newsletter: https://apophiss-newsletter-27c897.beehiiv.com/

If you want to support me or see posts of other projects that I have come over to: **buymeacoffee.com/mpetchinskg**
I post there daily several times a day

Get your Dinowicca or Christmas themed digital products, especially Santa Raptor songs and other musics. Here: **https://sg1fan23477.gumroad.com**

Apophis Yuletide Digital has not only digital Christmas items, but it will have all things with Dinowicca as well as other Digital products.

www.ingramcontent.com/pod-product-compliance
Lightning Source LLC
Chambersburg PA
CBHW020454180726
47992CB00027B/2618